Enid Blyton

STORIES OF

WIZARDS
AND
WITCHES

Look out for all of these enchanting story collections by
Enid Blyton

CHRISTMAS COLLECTIONS
Christmas Stories
Christmas Tales
Christmas Treats

SUMMER COLLECTIONS
Holiday Stories
Summer Holiday Stories
Summer Stories

OTHER COLLECTIONS
Brer Rabbit
Cherry Tree Farm
Fireworks in Fairyland
Mr Galliano's Circus
Stories of Wizards and Witches
The Wizard's Umbrella

Enid Blyton

STORIES OF
WIZARDS
AND
WITCHES

Hodder
Children's
Books

HODDER CHILDREN'S BOOKS

This collection first published in Great Britain in 2017 by Hodder and Stoughton

1 3 5 7 9 10 8 6 4 2

Enid Blyton ®
Enid Blyton's signature is a Registered Trademark of Hodder and Stoughton Limited
Text copyright © Hodder and Stoughton Limited, 2017
Illustrations © Hodder and Stoughton Limited, 2017

A CIP catalogue record for this book is available from the British Library.

ISBN 978 1 444 93997 2

Typeset in Caslon Twelve by Avon DataSet Ltd, Bidford-on-Avon, Warwickshire

Printed and bound in Great Britain by Clays Ltd, St Ives plc

The paper and board used in this book are made from wood from responsible sources

Hodder Children's Books
An imprint of
Hachette Children's Group
Part of Hodder and Stoughton
Carmelite House
50 Victoria Embankment
London EC4Y 0DZ

An Hachette UK Company
www.hachette.co.uk
www.hachettechildrens.co.uk

Contents

Too-Wise
the Wizard

Too-Wise the Wizard

TOO-WISE WAS a powerful wizard. He knew almost everything, and he had travelled in every country under the sun and moon. He had met witches and fairies, enchanters and magicians, and never had he found any wiser than himself.

So he grew proud and boastful. He built himself a wonderful palace right in the middle of Fairyland, and there he made his spells and did his magic. Clouds of enchantments always hung over the topmost pinnacle, and little elves scuttled by quickly at night, for they were afraid of the wizard.

Not very far away was the palace of the King and

Queen of Fairyland. They were angry to think that a wizard should come and live so near to them, but they could do nothing to prevent it.

One day Too-Wise decided to give a marvellous party, and invite to it all the witches, enchanters and magicians of the world. He had no right to do this, for they were not allowed in Fairyland unless the queen, Titania, gave permission. But little he cared for that!

The invitations were sent out. This was one of them:

TOO-WISE THE WONDERFUL WIZARD

INVITES

GREENEYE THE WITCH

TO

A PARTY AT HIS PALACE

(SPORTS.)

'What sort of sports is he going to have?' everyone wondered. 'None of the witches or wizards is very good at running and jumping. It can't be that.'

It wasn't. The sports that Too-Wise was going to have were quite different. They were competitions in magic. He meant to show everyone how clever he was, and to win all the prizes himself.

The King and Queen of Fairyland were worried about the party. They didn't like to think of all those witches and magicians in Fairyland. For, as you know, there are not very many good ones. So they put their heads together, and tried to think of a plan.

After they had thought for some time they decided that they couldn't stop the party. But they determined to send someone to it to watch all that happened, and report to them afterwards.

'We'll send Tippy the Elf,' they decided. 'He loves dressing up, and he is very sharp – he will notice everything.'

So they sent for Tippy the Elf, and told him what they wanted him to do. He was delighted, and clapped his hands gaily.

'What fun, what fun!' he cried. 'I'll make old Too-Wise think I am the greatest magician in the world!'

'But Tippy dear,' said the queen, 'you know this is rather a dangerous task we are setting you. If you are discovered, you may be spirited away and never heard of again!'

'I'll take the risk,' said Tippy, but he stopped clapping his hands, and looked rather thoughtful.

The great day came, and with it arrived all the guests of Too-Wise the Wizard. You should have seen them! Most of the witches came on broomsticks, which were gaily decorated with ribbons in honour of the party.

The enchanters chose all kinds of ways to come. Some arrived on the backs of eagles, and some on rosy clouds. Some came in golden carriages drawn by goblin slaves, and some made the wind bring them. One came unseen by anyone, and suddenly appeared with a bang just by Too-Wise, as he was standing at the top of the wide stairs, receiving his guests. It upset the wizard very much, and he gave the enchanter an angry glare.

'Not very polite,' he said, '*not* very polite!'

And what about Tippy the Elf? Well, he had decided to pretend that he wasn't much of a magician, and to come on his feet, for he didn't want Too-Wise to notice him too closely in case he found out that he was not really one of the guests.

So Tippy, in big pointed hat and flowing cloak, humbly walked up to the front door, and took off his boots in the hall, for it was a rainy afternoon. Then he went up the stairs and shook hands with Too-Wise. The wizard didn't take much notice of him, for just behind Tippy was a very famous witch, who had eyes in the back of her head as well as in the front, and Too-Wise was anxious to meet her.

Then there was tea. It was a wonderful meal. There was nothing on the table at all except empty plates, glasses and dishes, knives and forks and spoons.

Too-Wise sat at the head, and asked for silence.

'You have only to wish for what you would like,' he said, 'and I have arranged that it shall appear.'

Then my goodness, you should have seen the things that appeared, when all the guests wished! A chocolate cake as big as a drum sat in the middle, and a red, white and yellow jelly appeared at one end, and a pink blancmange shaped like just a house at the other. It was wonderful!

Sandwiches shot up from nowhere, and strawberry ices jumped into the waiting dishes. One witch, who had a liking for pickled onions, wished for a big jar of them, and they appeared just in front of her. But as it happened that the enchanter next to her hated the smell and sight of onions, they disappeared just as quickly – for he at once wished them away again!

The witch wished them back, and Tippy, who was just opposite, began to giggle when they disappeared again.

But he was hungry so he did a little wishing on

his own account, and was delighted to see a ginger cake and a cream bun appear side by side on his plate.

After tea all the guests went into the great hall of the palace, where the competitions were to be held.

First of all there was a competition to see who was the cleverest at turning into something else. Tippy got quite frightened as he watched, especially when one witch nearby changed very suddenly into a large cat, and scratched his leg.

This is no place for me, thought Tippy. *My turn will come soon, and I shall never be able to turn into anything, for I don't know the right magic. I had better hide.*

So he slipped behind a curtain, and watched the party through a little hole he made with his penknife.

Dragons and unicorns, lions and tigers, beetles and bears, pranced about the hall, and then changed back again into witches and wizards. Too-Wise looked at them all scornfully, and then, muttering some magic words, he suddenly turned into a seven-headed giant. Tippy began to tremble. He didn't like it a bit.

'I've won *that* competition!' said Too-Wise, changing back to himself again. 'Now let's get on with the next. Which of us has got the most wonderful thing in his possession?'

Tippy peered through his hole, and gaped to see all the marvellous things that were handed round. There was a needle that could sew by itself, a glass that could be filled with any liquid wished for by tapping the rim, and a rabbit that could sing. There was a hat which made the wearer invisible, and a cloak that made him handsome to look upon.

But Too-Wise brought out a mirror, and set it before the guests. 'Think of what you will, and it will appear in the mirror,' he said.

Then in the mirror came a curious succession of strange pictures, the thoughts of all the guests around. Tippy wished the Fairy Queen could see it, for he thought she would love it. As he thought that, he saw her picture appear in the mirror, and everyone exclaimed in surprise.

'Who dares to think of that silly queen at my party?' stormed Too-Wise. But everyone vowed that no thought of that kind had come into his or her mind, so the wizard said no more. But he wondered very much, and cast a sharp eye on all his guests to see if any of them were shams. It was well for Tippy then that he was behind the curtain!

'I have won this competition too,' said Too-Wise, boastfully. 'You will have to make me your king! Now for the third competition. You can each try and think of something I have never seen! Ho ho! If you can do that, I shall be surprised!'

Now all the guests were getting rather cross with Too-Wise. They thought it was a shame that he should win the prizes himself, and they certainly didn't want him to be their king. So they racked their brains to think of something he hadn't seen.

'Hurry up, hurry up,' said Too-Wise. 'There's nothing you can think of that I've not seen. You are stupid creatures compared to me, Too-Wise the

Wonderful Wizard!'

The witches and enchanters scowled at him. They would have liked to turn him into an earwig or something unpleasant like that, but they feared his power. They were terribly afraid, too, that he really *would* become their king, for he certainly was clever.

They began to ask him questions.

'Have you ever seen the star-shaped lamp that hangs in the deepest underground cave of the dwarfs?' asked one witch.

'Yes, and I've blown it out!' said Too-Wise, grinning.

'Have you ever seen the silver wand of the fairy who guards the Rainbow Path?' asked another witch. 'She keeps it locked up in a cupboard.'

'Yes, I have,' said Too-Wise. 'I stole her keys one day, and unlocked the cupboard to see the wonderful wand.'

'Have you seen the green wishing-carpet belonging to the Goblin King?' asked an enchanter, suddenly.

'It is said that none but he has ever cast eyes on it.'

'*I* have,' answered Too-Wise, puffing out his narrow chest. 'I gave him a spell he wanted, and in return he let me see his carpet.'

The witches and wizards sat silent for a moment. It seemed as if Too-Wise really *had* seen everything! Then a sharp-eyed one spoke.

'Have you seen the whistling fish belonging to the Prince of Dreamland?' he asked.

There was a pause, for none of the other enchanters had ever heard of this. But Too-Wise laughed.

'Ha ha!' he said. 'You're trying to catch me! The Prince has no such thing! I had dinner with him last week, and saw every one of his treasures – and there was no whistling fish!'

'You are right,' said the enchanter. 'I *was* trying to catch you, for you are too proud.'

'Have a care what you say!' said Too-Wise, frowning. 'If I become your king, I shall not forget those who treat me badly now.'

The game went on – but no one could find anything that Too-Wise had not seen. He sat there in front of them, vain and conceited, certain that he would become their king at the end of the party.

When the last witch and wizard had asked him their questions, there was a silence. Then Too-Wise stood up.

'I shall make myself your king,' he said. 'Not one of you is as wise as me.'

'We do not want a king,' said the guests. 'Least of all do we want you, oh, Too-Wise, Too-Vain, Too-Proud!'

'What!' cried the Wizard, in a rage. 'Well, think of something I have never seen, and I will disappear and never come back! But if you cannot, then I shall rule over you, and make you smart for these words!'

What would have happened next no one knows. But just as a witch was about to speak, someone near the curtain where Tippy was hiding moved back a step, and trod on the elf's toe.

'Ow!' cried Tippy in pain.

In a trice the curtain was dragged back, and the elf, in all his fine disguise of pointed hat and cloak, stood before the surprised company. He trembled, for he knew that things would go badly with him, now that he was discovered.

'So ho!' cried the witch who had pulled the curtain back. 'Who is this?'

Tippy stepped out, and tried to look bold.

'I am a great wizard,' he said. 'Beware of me!'

Too-Wise laughed.

'Then perhaps *you* can think of something I have never seen!' he said, mockingly. 'Try to think, or you will be turned into a droning fly. Quick!'

Tippy put his hands into his pockets, and wondered whatever he was to do. His right hand closed over a little red apple he had picked from his own apple tree that morning. And he suddenly thought of an idea.

'I will make all your guests laugh at you and your conceit,' said the elf boldly. 'Get ready to disappear for ever, oh Too-Wise!'

Everyone crowded around the elf, and Too-Wise scowled angrily.

'Speak,' he commanded Tippy.

The elf took the apple from his pocket, and placed it on the table.

'Have you ever seen the little brown pips in this apple of mine?' he asked, with a laugh.

Too-Wise stared at the apple in dismay. Such a simple question – but he could only answer 'No'! No one could see apple pips before the apple was cut. What was he to do? Everyone began laughing, and fingers were pointed mockingly at the wizard.

'It isn't fair,' said Too-Wise.

'Yes, it is,' said Tippy. 'You shouldn't have been so conceited, Too-Wise. Everyone heard you say that you would disappear for ever, if anybody could think of something you had never seen. Now, answer my question – have you ever seen the pips in my little apple?'

'Answer, answer!' cried all the witches and wizards.

'I have never seen them,' answered Too-Wise, and as he uttered those words there came a rushing wind, and it bore him away for ever. How the witches and wizards cheered when he went! They were so glad not to have him for king.

They went home immediately, and Tippy was left alone in the palace. His first action was to take the magic mirror that had belonged to Too-Wise, and hoist it on to his back. He meant to give it to the Queen as a present. Then he ran quickly out of the door. He was just in time. As he went down the steps there came a strange whistling sound. Tippy turned to see what was happening.

The wizard's castle suddenly changed into blue smoke, and streamed up into the sky. It was gone!

'Hurrah!' shouted Tippy, and staggered off to Titania with his heavy mirror. 'What an adventure! Three cheers for my little red apple!'

The Little
Pixie-Cat

The Little Pixie-Cat

ONCE UPON a time, Grubby the goblin did the Green Witch a good turn. In payment she gave him a little pixie-cat, and he carried it home in delight.

Now a pixie-cat is very valuable indeed, for it has plenty of magic in it. When it is exactly a year old it can turn all it sits upon to pure gold. Only just for that night, though, so that you must be sure to know the birthday of a pixie-cat or it is of no use to you.

Grubby the goblin was poor, and he was also very disagreeable. He was dirty and untidy, and none of his neighbours liked him, for he was always borrowing and never returning, always promising and never keeping his word.

So when they saw him carrying a pixie-cat home

one day they didn't rush out and say how pleased they were. They just stared in surprise, and said to one another, 'Ho! Grubby's got a pixie-cat! Perhaps he will wash himself for once on the cat's birthday!'

Grubby shut the cat in the cellar and went out to tell everyone of his good luck. He was angry that people didn't seem as glad as he wanted them to be. He went home frowning and scowling.

'Horrid things!' he said to himself. 'They are jealous of me! They know I shall soon be rich. Indeed, I'll be so rich that they'll have to make me chief of the village – and won't I punish them and pay them back for all the rude things they have said to me and thought of me!'

The pixie-cat's first birthday was in three days' time, and the goblin became very busy, for he meant to be as rich as possible. He collected three sacks – one of pennies, one of stones and one of dust. Then he took a cushion and put it right on top of the three sacks.

'Ha!' he said, pleased with his idea. 'On her birthday night the cat will sit on this cushion on top of these three sacks – and then when the clock strikes twelve the pennies will change to gold, the stones will be golden stones and the dust will be gold-dust, worth a fortune! Ho, I'll be richer than any goblin in the kingdom, and my, won't I make the people of this village sorry they ever looked down their noses at me!'

Now it was the custom for everyone in the village to be present on the first birthday of a pixie-cat, so that they might watch the wonderful magic working when the clock struck midnight. So Grubby the goblin sent out invitations, and at ten o'clock the people of the village began to arrive. There were pixies, brownies, gnomes, fairies and elves, and they all squeezed themselves into Grubby's little kitchen.

Grubby was there, and so was the pixie-cat, perched up high on her cushion, over the three sacks. Grubby hadn't provided any buns or lemonade – he was too mean. He just stood there and said, 'Good evening' when folk came in, but he didn't say, 'How do you do?' or, 'It's a fine night,' or anything polite and friendly. He really was an ill-mannered fellow.

At eleven o'clock everyone was there. Then Grubby began to talk. How he talked! How he boasted! And dear me, what a spiteful, mean little goblin he showed himself to be.

'Nobody's ever had a pixie-cat in this village except me!' he said. 'I'm going to be rich – richer than any of you. I shall build myself a new cottage with six rooms, and I shall have two servants. I shall give wonderful feasts to all the witches and goblins I know – but I shan't ask any of you to my feasts! No, I shall leave you out!'

'We shan't mind that, Grubby,' said a tall brownie. 'You don't wash your neck often enough for us to want to come to your parties!'

'Ho, is that you, Skinny the brownie?' cried the goblin fiercely. 'Well, let me tell you this – I'll buy your cottage when I'm rich, and I'll turn you out, you and all your children – so there!'

'You always were a mean fellow,' said an elf with long silver wings. 'You'll be more horrid than ever when you are rich!'

'You'll never be rich!' shouted Grubby angrily. 'You play about with butterflies and birds all day long, Silverwings! They can't do anything for you. Why don't you make friends with witches, as I do? Then maybe you would have a pixie-cat too, to make you rich.'

'We don't want to be rich,' said a gnome. 'We are quite happy as we are. Your gold won't make you any happier, Grubby; don't make any mistake about that. It won't make us like you any better, or be any more friendly. We'd rather be friends with a lame earwig than with a rich and unpleasant goblin like you!'

Grubby was so angry that he hardly knew what to say. For a while everyone sat silent, watching the hands of the clock creeping slowly round to midnight. The little pixie-cat began to purr loudly. She knew it was nearly time for her magic to work.

Grubby became excited as he saw the time getting so near. He began to talk again.

'When all these sacks hold gold,' he said, 'I shall buy a golden carriage and ride in it. I shall wear a cloak of silver cloth, and lace my shoes with golden laces. I shall ask the Great Wizard who lives in Towering Castle to visit me. And I will walk through the village with him, pretending not to see you.'

Grubby took up his walking-stick and pretended he was walking down the street, looking haughtily from side to side.

'When I meet any of you on the path, I shall say: "Get out of my way!",' he said, 'and if you don't move at once, I shall hit you with my stick! Like that! And like that!'

Grubby slashed about in the air with his stick, and the pixie-cat stopped purring in alarm. It was almost twelve o'clock, but Grubby still had one more thing to say.

'And the Great Wizard from Towering Castle will wave his stick round his head, and change you all into earwigs – like this!'

Grubby swung his stick sharply round his head and the end of it hit the little pixie-cat on the cushion! She gave a sharp mew, sprang fiercely at Grubby, and scratched his arm. Then she leapt out of the window and disappeared into the night. At the same moment the clock began to strike twelve!

'Oh, oh! I'm hurt! The pixie-cat's gone and it's midnight! Catch her, someone!' groaned the goblin. But nobody moved. Everyone was thinking exactly the same thought.

It serves Grubby the goblin right! they all thought. And so it did. Silently the little folk slipped out of the cottage and went home, leaving Grubby alone.

How ashamed he was! How he cried and groaned! He felt as if he couldn't possibly face anyone the next day, so he packed up his bag and went. Where he journeyed to, nobody knows, and nobody wants to know either!

As for that little pixie-cat, she went back to the Green Witch, and there she is still. The little folk saw the way she went, because all the stones and earth she ran on as the clock struck midnight changed into gold. They left the gold patches there as a warning to greedy goblins, and you can see them to this day — curious yellow spots in the ground, the size of a little cat's footprint!

The Strange
Umbrella

The Strange Umbrella

TIPTAP THE pixie lived in Apple-Tree Cottage in the very middle of Feefo Village. He had two nice little rooms, a kitchen and a bedroom, and outside the cottage was a pocket-handkerchief of a garden – very small, but quite enough for Tiptap to manage.

Now Tiptap was the only pixie in Feefo Village who did no proper work. He had five golden pounds a week of his own, which his old Aunt Tabitha Twinkle sent him, and he just made this do nicely. It bought him bread and butter, cocoa to drink, apple tarts from Mother Buttercup's shop, and fresh eggs from the egg-woman.

Everyone else in the village had their own work to do. The egg-woman looked after her hens and sold their nice brown eggs, the balloon-man sold balloons, Mother Buttercup made lovely cakes and tarts, and the bee-woman got honey from her bees and put it into pots. Everyone did something – except Tiptap, who was the laziest little pixie in the kingdom.

Now one day Tiptap went to see his Aunt Tabitha Twinkle, and she told him she had one or two little jobs for him to do to help her.

'There's my broom that wants mending,' she said. 'The handle has come off. And there's the garden gate that creaks terribly. You might stop it for me. Oh, and there's my stepladder too – something's gone wrong with it, Tiptap, and I'd be so glad if you'd see to it.'

'All right,' said Tiptap, rather crossly. He didn't want to mend things for his aunt. He wanted to sit in her nice new hammock and swing himself in the sun.

I'll just have a nice swing first, he thought to himself,

and he ran to the hammock. But, do you know, he hadn't been swinging in the sunshine for more than two minutes when he fell fast asleep!

He slept for two hours, and then he heard his aunt calling him in a very cross voice.

'Tiptap! Tiptap! Why haven't you done all I asked you to? There's the gate still creaking, the broom still broken, and the stepladder not mended! You are a very naughty pixie.'

Tiptap tumbled out of the hammock and ran to the garden shed. He took out the oil-can and ran to the gate to oil it – but he was in such a hurry that he put far too much oil down the hinges, and spilt a lot over the gate itself. He didn't trouble to rub it off with a rag, but left it there and ran to the broken broom.

Quickly he hammered a nail into the handle, and stuck the brush on. Then he looked at the stepladder. One of the rungs was unsafe, and Tiptap saw that it would need quite an hour's work to take out the bad rung and put in a nice new one.

'Bother!' said the pixie, crossly. 'I can't do that! I shall just stick the old rung in again and tell Aunt Tabitha Twinkle I have mended it. She will never know!'

And that is what the lazy little creature did. Then he ran to his aunt, and said, 'Did you call me, Aunt Tabitha? I have done all the jobs you asked me to, you know, so you really mustn't be so cross.'

'Oh, you're a good little pixie, then,' said his aunt, pleased. 'Come along in and have some pink jelly. It has just set nicely, and I know you're fond of it. Then I'll give you your five pounds and you shall go home.'

Tiptap sat down to eat the jelly. Just as he was finishing it, he saw his aunt's great friend, Mother Smiley-Face, coming in at the gate – and oh my! She had a fine new dress on, and the oil that Tiptap had left on the gate smeared itself all over the blue silk, and *what* a mess it made!

Mother Smiley-Face was very cross. She hurried

up to Aunt Tabitha Twinkle and showed her what had happened.

'There's my nice new dress all ruined!' she said. 'Whatever have you been doing to your gate?'

'Oh, that's Tiptap,' said Aunt Tabitha, crossly. 'He didn't wipe the gate clean after oiling it, I suppose!'

'I've come to ask you if you will let me see your new bonnet,' said Mother Smiley-Face, wiping her dress carefully.

'Oh, certainly!' said Aunt Tabitha, pleased. 'I'll fetch it for you. It's on the top of the wardrobe. Get me the stepladder, Tiptap.'

The pixie fetched the ladder, and his aunt climbed up to get her bonnet – but, oh dear me! When she stepped on the bad rung, it broke, and down she fell, clutching at the parcels on the wardrobe as she did so, so that a whole pile of them fell on the floor in a cloud of dust.

'Oh! Oh! You wicked little pixie! You haven't mended the ladder after all!' said Aunt Tabitha, angrily. 'Oh, I've hurt my knee – and look at all the mess!'

Mother Smiley-Face helped Aunt Tabitha up, and then fetched the broom to sweep up the mess – but of course the handle flew off as soon as she started sweeping, because Tiptap hadn't mended it properly.

'Well, look at that!' said Aunt Tabitha, now really angry. 'I asked you to do three little things for me, Tiptap, and see how you've done them! I'm ashamed of you! You don't deserve your five pounds a week! In future you shall only have two, and I shan't give you five again until I see that you know how to do a piece of work well.'

So Tiptap was given two pounds instead of five, and sent home in disgrace.

Each week after that only two golden pounds came for him instead of five, and soon Tiptap was in rather a bad way. He could manage to feed himself on two pounds, but if he needed anything new, he had no money to buy it. When his kettle suddenly grew a hole in it, he couldn't buy another. When his spade broke, he had no money for a new one. Of course, he could have mended them if he had set to work with a will, but he was a lazy fellow, and found it much easier to borrow from other folk instead.

So when things went wrong, Tiptap ran round to his friends.

'My clock has stopped and I can't set it going again,' he said to the egg-woman. 'Would you lend me one of yours, please?'

The egg-woman had two clocks, so she lent Tiptap one, thinking that when the pixie had mended his own, he would give hers back. But the lazy fellow didn't bother to try and mend his, now that he had got the egg-woman's.

When his kitchen lamp broke, he ran to Mother Buttercup, who had a spare one, and begged her to lend it to him.

'I'll soon mend mine,' he promised, 'and then you shall have yours back, Mother Buttercup.'

But, of course, *he* didn't trouble to mend his lamp, and poor Mother Buttercup had to go without her second one for weeks and weeks.

Soon Tiptap's cottage was full of things he had borrowed, and his garden shed full of things of his own that he had broken and that were waiting to be mended. But Tiptap didn't mend a single one. No – if people were kind enough to let him have things in their place, well, he would borrow and borrow and borrow!

Now one day he broke his umbrella. He looked at it, and saw that it would take him quite two hours to mend it properly.

'Oh bother!' said Tiptap. 'I'll go and borrow the balloon-man's. I know he has two.'

So he went to the balloon-man, and asked him to lend him his second umbrella, because it was raining very hard and he wanted to go out.

'I'm sorry,' said the balloon-man, 'but I lent my old one to my cousin yesterday, and I've only got my new one left. I can't lend you that, Tiptap, because I've got to go out selling balloons, and I must have an umbrella to keep the rain off me when I sit all day at my corner.'

Then Tiptap went to the bee-woman and asked her to lend him *her* umbrella. But she wouldn't.

'I've only got one, as you know very well, Tiptap,' she said. 'Also, I know that if I lent it to you, you wouldn't bring it back to me. You're getting a very bad name for borrowing, and you'd better stop doing it. Where's that kettle I lent you a month ago?'

Tiptap went red, said goodbye, and ran out. He tried to borrow an umbrella from Gobo the elf who lived in the next cottage, but Gobo had no umbrella at all.

'Now what am I to do?' wondered Tiptap, turning up his coat-collar, because the rain trickled down his neck. 'I do want to go and see Hey-Ho the gnome this morning, and I shall get so wet if I walk across the common without an umbrella!'

But since no one would lend him an umbrella, he

had to start off without one. He began to walk over the common, and he felt very cross, for the rain made him wetter and wetter.

Soon he came to Dame Trips's cottage, and he wondered if *she* would lend him an umbrella. So he ran up the garden path and popped his head in at the kitchen window.

'Could you lend me an umbrella?' he asked Dame Trips, who was busy setting out two cups of cocoa on a tray.

'No,' said Dame Trips. 'I haven't one to lend.'

Tiptap ran off again – but just as he passed the front door, what should he see standing outside in the porch but a fine umbrella! Goodness, it *was* a splendid one! It was red with big yellow spots all over it, and the handle was bright green. Instead of a little spike sticking out below the umbrella part, there was a funny knob in the shape of a little face.

'There! Dame Trips said she hadn't an umbrella, and she had, all the time! She told me a story!' said

Tiptap. 'I've a good mind to borrow that fine umbrella just to punish her! I can easily leave it here on my way home again.'

He went up to the umbrella. It certainly was a lovely one, the biggest and brightest Tiptap had ever seen. He picked it up and ran down the path with it.

When he was out of sight, he put it up over his head to keep off the rain. Ah, if Tiptap could have seen the little knob of a face at the top then! How it grinned and winked to itself!

Now the way to Hey-Ho's was towards the west, and Tiptap turned his steps there – but much to his astonishment he found that he couldn't make his legs walk that way! They seemed to want to walk in the opposite direction.

Then he heard a tiny, chuckling laugh, and he wondered where it came from.

It sounds as if it's above the umbrella somewhere, he thought, so he peeped over the edge of it and looked – and he saw that little grinning knob of a face, winking and blinking at him for all it was worth!

'Ooh!' said Tiptap, in a fright. 'Ooh! This umbrella's magic! I must throw it away at once, before it does me any harm!'

He tried to fling it from him, but dear me, he couldn't let go of the handle! It seemed to hold on to his hand! Tiptap tried to take his hand away, but he couldn't. The handle closed round his fingers and held him fast.

'Ooh!' said Tiptap, beginning to cry. 'It *is* magic! *Now* what's going to happen!'

He hadn't long to wait before he knew, for the umbrella suddenly began to bowl along towards the north-east, just as if a great wind was behind it. It pulled Tiptap along after it, and the poor little pixie found himself running fast over the common, unable to do anything else. The big red umbrella pulled him along at a tremendous pace, and Tiptap was soon out of breath – but he *couldn't* let go of the handle.

'Where's it taking me to?' he wondered, the tears

pouring down his cheeks in fright. 'Oh dear! It can't have belonged to Dame Trips after all. It must have belonged to someone who was visiting her! Oh, why did I take it?'

At last, after taking Tiptap about five miles over hill and dale, the umbrella came to a little white house set on a hillside. On the gate was a name – Wizard Ho-Hum's Cottage.

Then Tiptap was more afraid than ever. He knew that the wizard would be very angry to find his umbrella had been taken from Dame Trips, for he would have to walk home in the rain.

The umbrella took Tiptap to the front door, and there it stayed. There didn't seem to be anyone in the house at all. Wizard Ho-Hum was out. He had gone to see his sister, Dame Trips – and my goodness, when he came out and found that someone had taken his umbrella, what a rage he was in.

'Well, I shall find the thief outside my front door, waiting for me!' he said to himself. 'My umbrella will be sure to take him there! But just look at this rain! How wet I shall get!'

So he did, for the rain poured down as he went across the common. When he at last got home, he was in a fine temper. He saw the umbrella by his front door, the handle still holding fast to Tiptap's hand, and the little head at the top chuckling and laughing for all it was worth.

'Ho!' he shouted, frowning angrily at Tiptap. 'So *you're* the thief, are you?'

'Please, no,' said Tiptap, in a small voice. 'I thought it was Dame Trips's umbrella, and I just borrowed it.'

'*I've* heard all about you!' said the wizard. 'You're the nasty, horrid little fellow that breaks your own things and goes about borrowing other people's and never takes them back again! Well, *I* call that stealing! Yes, I do! I'll teach you to steal *my* umbrella!'

He opened his front door, took the umbrella away from Tiptap's hand, and closed it. Then he stood it in a corner, and ordered Tiptap to go in.

'Now, I want a handyman,' he said to the frightened pixie. 'You can choose what you will do – either I take you to Pop-Off the policeman, and tell him you stole my umbrella, or *you* can be my handyman for six weeks, and do all my odd jobs till my other man comes back. If you try to run away, the red umbrella will come after you and catch you. Now, which will you choose?'

'P-p-p-please, I'll b-b-b-be your handy-m-m-m-man!' stammered the pixie, who couldn't bear the idea of being taken to Pop-Off.

'Then make yourself useful straight away!' commanded Ho-Hum. 'Take a pail and clean all the windows. Then peel some potatoes and prepare dinner for me.'

Tiptap set to work. How he made those windows shine! Then he peeled the potatoes, and put a milk pudding into the oven. After that the wizard made him chop wood till his arms ached.

What a time the pixie had for the next few weeks!

He was up at daybreak, and he wasn't allowed to go to bed till he had finished every single job there was to be done. He had to keep the cottage clean and tidy, cook all the meals, work in the garden, chop the wood and mend anything that got broken, for the wizard wouldn't hear of buying or borrowing fresh things.

Once Tiptap made up his mind to run away, and in the night he crept out of the cottage – but he hadn't gone very far before he heard a little chuckle behind him, and, oh my! In the moonlight what should he see but that red umbrella just behind him! It opened itself all of a sudden and the handle caught hold of Tiptap's hand. Then he was dragged all the way back to Ho-Hum's.

The wizard found him outside the front door in the morning, held tightly by the umbrella.

'Ho, so you thought you'd try to run away, did you?' he said. 'Well, you shall be punished for that!'

So Tiptap's day's work was twice as hard as before.

When he had been at Ho-Hum's for a month, he

found that he began to like his work. It was fun to make the cottage shine like a new pin. It was lovely to dig in the garden in the sun. It was exciting to mend something that was broken and make it as good as new again. Really, Tiptap quite enjoyed himself, and he began to sing and whistle at his work like a blackbird in spring.

'Ah, you're beginning to see that it is a fine thing to work!' said Ho-Hum one morning. 'What a nasty, lazy, good-for-nothing fellow you used to be, to be sure! See how clever your hands are, when you set them to something. Why, I shall be quite sorry to lose you tomorrow, when my old handyman comes back.'

'Is he coming back tomorrow?' asked Tiptap in dismay. 'Oh! I *shall* be sorry to go! It *will* seem funny going back home with nothing to do.'

'Well, since you're such a good hand at mending and making,' said Ho-Hum, 'why don't you make yourself the handyman of Feefo Village? I hear there isn't one there, and I'm sure folk would be very glad of one.'

'That's a splendid idea!' said Tiptap, pleased. 'Hurrah! I'll soon show everyone I'm not lazy or good-for-nothing!'

The next day Ho-Hum's old handyman came back, and Tiptap said goodbye to the wizard, who gave him a little tie-pin in the shape of a red umbrella, to remind him never to be lazy again. Tiptap stuck it proudly into his tie and marched home.

As soon as he got to Apple-Tree Cottage, and had set it in order again, he went to his garden shed. There were all the dozens of things he had broken and put there weeks before. He set to work to mend them, and by the end of the week there were all his tools, pots and pans, and everything else as good as new. Then Tiptap took back all the things he had borrowed, thanked the people who had kindly lent them to him, and said he was sorry he had kept them so long.

'I'm going to set up as handyman to the village,' he

told everyone. 'Let me have anything broken or spoilt, and I'll mend it for you for a penny or two. I want to do something for my living now!'

How astonished and pleased all the people were! They let Tiptap have all their broken things and he mended them splendidly. Soon he had quite a lot of money in his purse, and wasn't he proud of it!

Then one day his Aunt Tabitha came to see him, to give him all the pounds he hadn't had whilst he had been away.

'You shall have five pounds a week again now!' she said, when she found out how hard Tiptap was working, and how changed he was. But Tiptap wouldn't take a penny!

'No, thank you, Aunt Tabitha Twinkle,' he said. 'I've found out that it is a hundred times nicer to earn money myself than to take it from someone else for doing nothing. Please keep it yourself, or give it to the Hospital for Sick Brownies. In future I'm going to work hard and be happy.'

He kept his word, and his Aunt Tabitha Twinkle sent the money to the Brownie Hospital, which was very much delighted to have it. As for Tiptap, you should hear him whistle and sing as he mends pots and pans and sharpens knives. It really is lovely to listen to him. He still has his tie-pin, and he wouldn't part with it for the world!

'That was the best thing that ever happened to me!' he often says. 'I'll never be sorry that strange umbrella took me away!'

Redcap and the
Broomstick Witch

Redcap and the Broomstick Witch

THERE WAS once a little gnome called Redcap, who lived right in the middle of Cuckoo Wood. His cottage was the cosiest little place, surrounded by trees and wild flowers. Redcap thought he was the luckiest little gnome in the world.

Early one morning he rang the little bell up on his roof to wake his friends for breakfast. Out of their holes peeped the bunnies. Squirrels scampered down from the trees.

The blackbirds and starlings came, and the robins and sparrows flew round, whistling and chirping.

Redcap gave them crumbs to eat and water to drink.

He picked two of his finest lettuces for the bunnies, and gave the squirrels some nuts.

Then they sat in a ring and told each other the dreams they had had in the night.

When it came to Redcap's turn, he looked rather upset.

'I had a *horrid* dream last night,' he said. 'All about the Broomstick Witch. I dreamt I was taken prisoner, and I couldn't escape!'

'Never mind,' said Spindly, the starling. 'It was only a dream. It won't come true, Redcap. The Broomstick Witch wouldn't *dare* to come here.'

'And if she did trap you,' said Perky the squirrel, 'we'd rescue you somehow.'

Redcap felt better. After all, it *was* only a dream. He decided not to worry about it any more.

He ate breakfast with his friends, and soon forgot about the dream.

Later, Redcap was cooking dinner, when he heard someone walking through the wood calling out:

'Brooms for sale! Brooms for sale! Nice new brooms for sale!'

He peeped out of his window and saw an old woman with a shawl, walking up the path to his cottage.

Redcap remembered his dream. Perhaps this was the witch. Oh dear, oh dear!

Never mind! he thought. *She can't harm me here. Anyway, she doesn't look like a witch.*

The old woman stopped at his window. 'Would you like a nice new broom?' she asked.

'No, thank you,' answered Redcap, though it wasn't *quite* the truth, for he did need a new broom. He didn't want to buy one from an old woman who might be a witch though. You never knew what spell she might leave behind.

The old woman sighed, and put the brooms over her shoulder again. Then she sniffed at the smell of Redcap's soup.

'Oh!' she said. 'How delicious that smells! I am so hungry, and I've sold no brooms today.'

Well, thought Redcap, *it can't do any harm to give her some soup*. He called her inside.

When she had eaten her meal, the old woman thanked Redcap, got up, and went on her way with her load of broomsticks. Later, when Redcap went outside he stared in astonishment – for leaning against his gate was a brand new broom!

Redcap took it and swept his garden path. It was a fine broom, and swept as clean as could be.

'Perky! Spindly! Bobtail!' called Redcap joyfully. 'Come and see what I've got!'

All his friends gathered round.

'Where did you get it?' asked Perky. 'From the old witch woman?'

'She can't be an old witch woman,' said Redcap, 'or she wouldn't have been so kind as to give me a fine new broom in return for the bowl of soup I gave her.'

'I didn't like her,' said Perky.

'Nor did we,' said the others.

'Don't be silly!' laughed Redcap. 'See what a fine broom it is, and see how well it sweeps!'

He began to sweep his path again – but oh dear! What do you think happened?

The broom suddenly rose in the air and flew away with Redcap!

'Oh!' he cried. 'It's magic! It's taking me to the Broomstick Witch!'

'Perky! Climb to the treetops and follow him!' called Bobtail the rabbit to the little squirrel. Perky leapt into the nearest tree, and soon was lost from sight.

'I *knew* she was a horrid old woman!' sighed Bobtail. 'Poor Redcap! Whatever can we do?'

'We must wait until Perky comes back,' said Spindly. So they waited, feeling very worried.

After a whole hour had gone by, Perky returned, out of breath.

'I followed the broom!' he panted, 'and I've never travelled so fast in my life! It's gone to Red Chimney

Cottage on Witchy Hill. It flew down to the garden, and as soon as it touched the ground, that old witch woman came out and tied poor Redcap up. Then she took him indoors and I came back here!'

'Dear, dear!' said Bobtail. 'We must rescue him. We promised we would if anything happened to him.'

'Let's go and hide near Red Chimney Cottage,' said Spindly. 'We might find some way to save him tonight, when the witch is out.'

So when the sun had set the little band of birds and bunnies set out, guided by Perky, who knew the way.

At last they arrived at Witchy Hill, and in the darkness crept up towards Red Chimney Cottage. They hid themselves carefully beneath cabbage leaves and waited. After a while the cottage door opened and the witch came out. She locked the door and put the key in her pocket. Then she jumped on her broomstick and rode off.

Quickly Redcap's friends ran out from their hiding

places and went up to the cottage door.

'Redcap! Redcap!' called Perky. 'Are you in there?'

'Yes!' answered Redcap. 'Oh! I *am* so glad to hear you. The witch has tied me up to keep me prisoner. She wants me to help her with her bad spells, and I won't.'

'Don't worry,' said Bobtail. 'We'll save you. We just need to find a way to get in.'

They tried the door, but it was locked tight.

'Try the window!' said Redcap.

Perky jumped up on the windowsill, but there were strong bars, and no one could get in or out *that* way.

Everyone was very worried.

'We *must* do something soon, or the witch will be back!' said Perky. 'Let's all think hard!'

'I know!' cried Bobtail. 'What about going down the chimney? Look, there's a tree that hangs over the roof, Perky. Couldn't you climb up, and pop down the chimney? There's no fire tonight, for the chimney isn't smoking.'

'Good idea!' cried Perky, scurrying up the tree. 'I'll nibble Redcap's ropes in two and he will soon be free!'

In no time the little squirrel was down the chimney. He ran to where Redcap lay in a corner, tied tightly up with ropes. How glad he was to see Perky!

'Now for a good nibble!' said the squirrel, and began gnawing at the ropes as hard as he could.

One by one they fell apart, and soon Redcap was free!

'Oh! thank you, Perky,' he said. 'Now, how can I get out?'

He looked around in a dreadful panic, then spotted the witch's spell-book, and magic wand on the shelf. He took the big book down, put it on the table and opened it. He found the spell he needed, and turning to face the door, said:

'Abracadabra, quick as can be, please unlock this door for me!'

At once, the door sprang open! All his friends outside crowded round him in delight.

'Come home quickly,' they said, 'before the witch comes back.'

'Hold on,' said Redcap. 'I have an idea.'

He went back inside and brought out all the brooms he could find.

'Listen!' he said. 'A witch is no good without her brooms. Take one each and sit on it. There are enough brooms for everyone but me.'

'But we can't leave you behind, Redcap!' cried everyone.

'You won't have to!' said the gnome, chuckling. 'I shall hide in the garden till the witch comes back. When she gets off *her* broom and goes inside, I shall take it quickly, say the magic rhyme, and off we'll all go as quick as lightning, leaving her behind!'

'What a splendid idea!' cried Bobtail. 'Then she'll be harmless, and we'll all get a good ride home. What fun!'

'Sh! Sh!' suddenly said Perky. 'She's coming! Hide quickly!'

They took the broomsticks to the long grass. Redcap hid among some hollyhocks near the door, and waited.

Down flew the witch on her broomstick, and landed by the door.

She jumped off and leant it up against the wall just near Redcap. Then she felt in her pocket to find the key. At the same moment Redcap gave a tremendous yell, snatched the broom and jumped on it. His friends did the same, and the witch fell over backwards in fright.

'Broomstick, fly
Away to the sky;
High and then low,
Away we go!'

As Redcap sang these magic words the broomsticks rose in the air and flew to Cuckoo Wood. The old witch called them, but they wouldn't go back to *her* any more!

When the friends arrived home after a fine ride, they chuckled in delight to know their little friend was safe once more. Redcap thanked them again and again.

'Now put your broomsticks in a heap,' he said, 'and we'll burn them. Then the old witch can do no more harm!'

The broomsticks were so full of magic that as they burnt the flames were green and the smoke was red.

Then the friends went to bed, and settled down happily to sleep, knowing they would have breakfast together in the morning, and they didn't need to worry about the Broomstick Witch any more!

Bobadil Becomes
a Wizard

Bobadil Becomes a Wizard

BOBADIL WAS a pixie, and a very smart one, too. He knew how many beans made five, and how much a pennyworth of sweets cost, and all the rest of the things taught at a good pixie school.

But he couldn't seem to find any work to do, now that he had left school, and was all on his own. Nobody wanted him, and Bobadil was getting very much upset about it.

I shall have to leave this town, and try somewhere else, thought Bobadil at last. So he packed up his things, put them in a big red handkerchief, slung them over his back, and set out.

He hadn't gone very far, before he saw a great crowd of pixies and gnomes standing at the street corner, talking very excitedly.

'What's the matter?' asked Bobadil.

'Oh, haven't you heard?' said one. 'Why, the great enchanter, Thinkalot, is passing through here this afternoon, and we all want to see him.'

Well, Bobadil thought he really must stop and see Thinkalot, so he popped his bundle down, and climbed up a lamppost. No sooner had he done that than he heard the sound of trumpets, and round the corner came a magnificent carriage, drawn by six white donkeys. In the carriage sat the enchanter Thinkalot, frowning hard at a book he was reading, and taking no notice at all of any of the cheering people.

'My, isn't he grand!' cried everyone, tremendously impressed. 'Just look at him, reading his magic books, and sitting there so grand and powerful!'

Bobadil thought the enchanter was wonderful, and he wished with all his heart that he could be an enchanter too, instead of an out-of-work pixie. He slid down the lamppost, and ran after the carriage, determined to follow it until it was out of sight.

On went the six white donkeys, trotting the carriage along at a smart pace, and on went Bobadil, fixing his eyes on the enchanter's tall, black hat, and star-patterned robe. He thought he looked tremendously grand, and the little pixie longed to have a hat and robe just exactly the same.

If I were dressed like that, he thought, *I should be able to get plenty of work, for people wouldn't dare to refuse me!*

He ran along after the carriage, which gradually drew ahead of him, and was soon away in the distance. Bobadil still ran on, keeping his eyes on the cloud of dust that was now all he could see of the enchanter's carriage.

He wasn't looking at all where he was going, so it

wasn't surprising that he suddenly tripped over something and fell bump, on to his little turned-up nose. He picked himself up, dusted his coat, and looked to see what it was that he had fallen over. It was a book! A great big red and black book, and on the front was written: *Thinkalot's Magic Book*.

'Oh my!' said Bobadil. 'The enchanter's own book of magic! It must have fallen out of the carriage. I say! What a find!'

He opened the book curiously, and looked inside. To his great astonishment, the same thing was written on every single page!

'Take this book back to its owner. Take this book back to its owner.' That was what Bobadil read ever so many times.

How can I take it back? wondered Bobadil. *The enchanter is miles away by now. I shouldn't have thought it was of much use anyhow, with just that one sentence written in it!*

He put the book under his arm, and went on his

way again. He hadn't gone very far before he saw a cloud of dust in the distance, that became bigger as he watched.

'Something's coming this way,' said Bobadil to himself. He watched to see what it was, and was very much surprised to see that it was the enchanter's carriage coming slowly back again, with the enchanter leaning out of it, looking closely at every piece of road he passed.

'Oho!' said Bobadil. 'He's missed his magic book. What a grand man he looks to be sure!'

The enchanter stopped when he saw Bobadil and spoke to him.

'Have you seen a big magic book?' he asked.

'Here it is,' said Bobadil, taking it from under his arm. 'It's a funny sort of book, I must say! It's got no magic in it at all.'

The enchanter smiled. 'Oh yes, it has,' he said. 'But you couldn't see it. Look now, whilst I hold it in my own hand.'

Bobadil looked at the page that the enchanter showed him, and to his surprise saw that now it was full of curious drawings, and wonderful magic words that he had never heard of.

'My!' he cried. 'That's a funny thing.'

'What would you like as a reward for finding my book?' asked the enchanter.

'Oh!' said Bobadil, most excited. '*I* know what I'd like, Sir Enchanter.'

'Speak on,' said Thinkalot.

'I'd like to have a tall black hat, and star-patterned robe like yours,' said Bobadil. 'You do look so very grand!'

'Very well,' said Thinkalot. 'You may have them.'

He said no more, but turned his donkeys round again, and drove quickly off, leaving Bobadil staring after him in surprise.

'Hie, hie,' cried the pixie, seeing the enchanter rapidly driving away. 'You haven't given me those clothes.'

The enchanter made no reply, and Bobadil felt dreadfully disappointed. He began to run after the carriage when he suddenly tripped, and down he went again, head over heels.

'Now, what tripped me up *that* time?' wondered Bobadil crossly. He sat up and looked – and he saw that he had tumbled over a long robe that wrapped him about from his head to his heels – a star-patterned robe, just like the enchanter's.

'*There's* magic for you!' said Bobadil in astonishment. 'Have I got a big black hat, too?'

He felt to see, and yes, he had, set on the top of his little round head.

'Ha,' said the pixie, getting on to his feet again. 'I'm very grand now, I am. I'll make everyone think I am a great wizard, and if I can't get a job to do now, well, I'll eat my fine new hat.'

He decided to go straight on, and take the road to Twisty-Town, a little place a good way off, that would not have heard either of Bobadil the pixie or Thinkalot the Enchanter.

On his journey, Bobadil meets a large brown rabbit who offers to carry him to Twisty-Town on his back. When they arrive, they are told about a bag of gold that has gone missing and Bobadil uses his cunning to catch the thief. The townspeople are convinced that only a real wizard could have solved the mystery and give him some of the gold as a reward. Bobadil and his friend the rabbit are delighted and continue their journey.

Read on for their next adventure . . .

The Gobble-Up
Witch

The Gobble-Up Witch

BOBADIL TRAVELLED on for some time until he came to another town. To his surprise, as he rode through it nobody came to follow him. The houses were tightly shut, the windows were closed, and not a child or dog was in the streets.

'This is strange,' said Bobadil. 'Where is everyone on this fine day? Surely not shut up in their houses.'

He went to one house and knocked. There was no answer. He knocked again. Still no one came. He called. That made no difference either.

Bobadil went to all the houses in the street and

rang the bells and knocked – but nobody opened the door or even looked out of the window.

'Hey!' called Bobadil. 'Where is everybody? Is there no one here who can give a visitor a drink of water?'

For a minute there was no answer. Then a voice, frightened and shaking, came from one of the houses.

'Who are you?'

'I am Bobadil, the great wizard, who has just come from discovering the thief in Twisty-Town,' answered Bobadil in surprise.

A door opened cautiously and the head of an old gnome peeped out.

'You are not the witch Gobble-up in some new form?' he asked.

'Good gracious, no!' said Bobadil. 'Can't you see I am a wizard? Look at my hat and robe. What's the matter with everyone here?'

As he spoke, doors began to open up and down the street, and people began to creep out and come near to where Bobadil stood.

'I will tell you why we are so frightened,' said the old gnome. 'Our town is in the power of a horrible witch, and she has taken to eating some of us, or catching us as her servants. She is so clever that we never know when or how she is coming. She may come in the form of a horse, or a man, a rabbit, or even a stream of water. Whatever she touches on her way through the town becomes hers. So you see, when we see any stranger coming, we go into our houses, shut our doors, and wait for the witch to pass.'

'Well, I am no witch,' said Bobadil. 'I am a wizard.'

'Do you know of any spell to get rid of a wicked witch?' asked the old gnome hopefully.

'I might,' said Bobadil. 'Where does she live?'

Just as he asked that there came a shout of terror and the people began to run for their lives.

'See!' cried the gnome. 'She is coming now and in her own shape. Run, Sir Wizard.'

Bobadil didn't run, although he felt very like it.

He stayed where he was, and watched the witch come down the street on her broomstick. She was a hideous old woman, with bright green eyes and a very hooked nose.

'Good day to you, witch,' said Bobadil.

'Good day to yourself,' said the witch, stopping. 'I see you are a wizard?'

'And a very powerful one, too,' put in the rabbit, bravely.

'Ho, is that so?' said the witch. 'Can you change yourself into a roaring dragon?'

'Can *you*?' said Bobadil.

'Of course I can,' said the witch.

'Go on, then,' said Bobadil.

At once the witch turned into a fierce dragon, whose hot breath blew on to Bobadil and singed his hair.

'Wonderful, wonderful!' he cried. 'But pray turn into a witch again. You have set fire to my cloak with your burning breath.'

The dragon became a witch again, and laughed

to see the hem of Bobadil's cloak smouldering. She reached her hand up in the air, and brought it down with a can of water in it, much to Bobadil's astonishment. He took it, and splashed a little on to his cloak to put the smouldering out.

'Ha!' said the witch. 'Can you change yourself into a giant?'

'Can *you*?' asked Bobadil, nervously.

'Watch and see,' answered the witch, and straightaway turned herself into a giant as high as the clouds, so that Bobadil had to lie down to see the great pink face, away up in the sky above him.

'Marvellous! Marvellous!' cried Bobadil. 'Change back into a witch again!'

The giant became old witch Gobble-up, and she grinned at him.

'Now let me see *you* do something!' she said.

'In a minute,' said Bobadil, 'I will do something that you cannot do.'

'What is that?' asked the witch in surprise.

'I will change myself into an egg!' said Bobadil.

'Pooh, that's easy!' said the witch, scornfully. 'Look at me!'

Bobadil looked, and before his eyes she changed into a hen's brown egg, lying on the floor at his feet. In a flash Bobadil stooped down to pick it up and smash it, hoping that would put an end to the witch once and for all. But she was too quick for him. In a second she changed back to her own form again and stood glaring at Bobadil.

'What do you want to pick that egg up for?' she asked, angrily.

'To examine such a marvel closely, of course,' answered Bobadil. 'I know *one* thing you couldn't change yourself into, old witch, and that is a blade of grass! Such a small thing is more difficult to turn into than a big thing, and I'm sure that is beyond your powers.'

The witch snorted, said a quick magic word and changed into a green blade of grass. Like a flash the rabbit pounced, and Bobadil saw him chewing hard.

Ah, that's finished her, he thought, but alas! Just as he was going to pat the rabbit on the back, the witch reappeared.

'Punish your rabbit, punish your rabbit!' she cried. 'He tried to eat me, and if he hadn't picked the wrong blade of grass, I should be dead by now. Quick, punish your rabbit.'

Bobadil hardly had time to think what to do, but he just managed to.

'Wicked rabbit!' he said, turning to the frightened bunny. 'We will roast you over a fire, and cook you for our dinner now. Witch, turn yourself into a fire, and you shall yourself roast this wicked rabbit!'

The cruel witch laughed to hear this and at once changed into a roaring fire. Quick as thought, Bobadil snatched up the jug of water he had used to put out the smouldering of his robe, and poured it all over the fire. It fizzled – died down – and went out. Nothing was left of it but a few black embers. Bobadil and the rabbit waited tremblingly to see if the witch would come back to life again – but she didn't!

'She's dead, she's dead!' cried the rabbit, and flung his front paws round Bobadil's neck.

When the people heard this they all came flocking out of their houses again and made a cheering ring round the clever pair. They took them to the market and gave them the finest dinner there that they had ever had.

'Never have we seen such a clever wizard before,' they cried. 'Give him a bag of gold and bid him good luck on his way. He has saved us from the wicked witch.'

Well, Bobadil was very pleased to take the bag of gold they gave him and add it to the other gold he had had from the folk of Twisty-Town. He said goodbye to the people and once again he and the rabbit started on their travels to make their fortunes.

Mr Woff and
the Enchanter

Mr Woff and
the Enchanter

MR WOFF lived in a big house right in the middle of the village of Trim. He was the head-man, and everyone admired him, for he was wise and good. His village was the best and the prettiest in the whole of the land. The gardens were full of flowers, the roads were well kept and the little shops were merry and neat.

Mr Woff was very proud of his village indeed. He talked about it wherever he went, and told everyone what a fine healthy place it was to live in, how all the flowers grew so well, and how nice the people were.

One day he went to a grand party at the king's

palace, and found himself sitting next to a tall man in a pointed hat. This man looked rich, and he had piercing green eyes and a very deep voice. Mr Woff didn't know who he was, but he began to talk about his precious village just as he always did.

The tall, green-eyed man listened hard and seemed most interested.

'Dear me!' he said, after a while. 'Your village of Trim sounds delightful. I've a good mind to come and live there. I'm selling my castle on Tiptop Hill and I'm looking for a nice quiet place to build another in.'

Mr Woff was pleased to hear this. It would be grand to have someone building a castle in the village of Trim! He would make friends with the owner and would soon be very grand himself. Oho! He rubbed his hands, delighted.

But he wasn't quite so delighted when he heard who the green-eyed man was. No – his face fell and he looked quite frightened.

'That's the horrid enchanter, Too-Sly!' whispered a

friend of Mr Woff's to him, at tea-time. 'Whatever do you want to tell him about our village for? It would be simply dreadful if he came to live there! Why, he would frighten the children, make horrid spells, bring his nasty imp-servants with him, and turn our nice, peaceful little village into a dreadful, noisy place! He's had to sell his castle on Tiptop Hill because people complained about him so. I'm sure *we* don't want him in our dear little village!'

Mr Woff stared at his friend in horror. What! Had he really been talking to the enchanter Too-Sly? Oh dear, why couldn't he stop talking about his village of Trim to everyone? Now Too-Sly would be sure to come and live there. He would build his castle there, and turn the whole village upside-down in no time!

'But perhaps he *won't* come after all,' said Mr Woff. 'Perhaps I shall get another chance to talk to him and then I'll say there's no room for anyone else in Trim Village.'

Poor Mr Woff didn't get another chance to speak to the enchanter, though he tried very hard. He left the party feeling miserable, and went back home, hoping and hoping that that was the last he would hear of Too-Sly.

But it wasn't! The very next week there came a short fat man to the village of Trim, attended by two nasty little imps. He walked all over the village and at last came to the hill behind it. He had a good look at the hill and then asked someone who owned it.

'Mr Woff owns all this village,' said the little girl, half frightened at being spoken to by a man with two imps behind him. 'He lives down in the village, in that big house, there.'

The fat man went to Mr Woff's house and knocked at the door, *blim, blam*! Mr Woff opened the door.

'I've come to buy that hill behind this village, for my master, the great enchanter Too-Sly,' said the little fat man. 'My master will come tonight and stay with you, to pay you for the hill. Will you please get all the papers ready, so that we can start building his castle tomorrow?'

Mr Woff didn't know *what* to say! He was so upset, so startled to think that the castle was to be begun the very next day. Whatever could he do to stop it?

The little fat man gave Mr Woff a few papers, bowed and went down the path. Mr Woff shut the door with a bang and sat down on a hall chair, pale and troubled.

How dreadful to think that because he boasted about his dear little village of Trim, Too-Sly was going to live there and make it a horrid place for the villagers! Whatever could he do?

His little wife, Twinkle, came up to him, surprised to find Mr Woff sitting all alone in the hall. When he told her what had happened she was in despair.

'We must stop him coming!' she said.

'But how?' groaned Mr Woff.

'We must frighten him!' said Twinkle.

'Frighten a great enchanter like Too-Sly?' said Mr

Woff. 'Don't be silly. It can't be done!'

Twinkle went off to the kitchen to prepare a supper for the enchanter's coming. Mr Woff still sat on the hall chair, thinking. If only he *could* frighten Too-Sly! He knew that the enchanter would never live anywhere if he thought there was someone more powerful than he was, living in the same place. How could Mr Woff make the enchanter think he was even stronger than Too-Sly?

He thought and thought – and slowly a plan came to him. It was a strange plan, and Mr Woff wasn't sure that it would work. He thought he had better tell it to Twinkle, so off he went to the kitchen.

'I want to frighten the enchanter, as you said,' began Mr Woff. 'I want him to think I am a very strong and powerful man, so I've thought of a plan, Twinkle.'

'Oh, do tell me!' said Twinkle, mixing a cake quickly.

'Well – I'm going to put the cow in the cellar,' said Mr Woff. 'And I'm going to put the pig in the pantry. And I'm going to buy twenty tin trays and get my friend Jinks to come and drop them in the kitchen every five minutes!'

Twinkle stopped mixing the cake and stared at Mr Woff in alarm and surprise.

'Are you quite mad?' she cried. 'Whatever do you mean?'

'Wait, wait!' said Mr Woff, grinning all over his good-tempered face. 'Now, listen. When the pig grunts, as he is sure to do in the small pantry, I shall say that that is a wizard I have got prisoner, snoring in his sleep. When the cow bellows, as she will do, in that dark cellar, I shall say it is a dragon roaring down below, which I captured for a riding horse last week. And when Jinks keeps dropping the twenty trays in the kitchen, I shall say that is my giant servant, rattling his chains as he walks about the kitchen. Ho ho, that will make old Too-Sly shiver in his shoes!'

'Oh, Mr Woff, how clever you are!' cried his little wife. 'If Too-Sly thinks you've captured a dragon, taken a wizard prisoner, and keep a giant for a servant, he will be very much afraid of you. And perhaps he will go away and never come back!'

Mr Woff went off to buy the trays, very pleased with himself indeed. He called in and told his friend Jinks what he wanted him to do that night. Jinks was delighted, for he was always ready to play a joke.

'You can climb up the kitchen steps every five minutes or so,' said Mr Woff. 'Then you can drop all the twenty trays from the top, down to the stone floor. My, they *will* make a noise!'

Then Mr Woff went to get his old cow, and to her great surprise he led her down to the dark cellar.

Then he filled his little pantry with straw, threw a few pieces of turnip and carrot into the straw and fetched his great pig. He locked it in the pantry and the fat beast stared round in surprise at his new sty! He couldn't understand it at all.

Mr Woff changed into his best suit, and then waited impatiently for Too-Sly to arrive. At half past six a golden carriage rolled up to his gate and out stepped Too-Sly the enchanter, in a hat even taller and more pointed than he had worn before, and in a cloak that swept the ground as he walked. He looked very grand, very powerful, and poor little Mr Woff couldn't help wondering what would happen to him if Too-Sly found out the tricks he was going to play on him!

The supper was laid on the table. It was a very good supper indeed. There were plenty of pies, a great joint of roast ham, six different puddings and ice cream to finish up with. Too-Sly was greedy and he was pleased to see such a spread.

He and Mr Woff and Twinkle sat down to the meal. Too-Sly soon began to talk about the castle he meant to build. It was to spread all over the hill, and Too-Sly said that he wanted twenty servants from the village to help him. Mr Woff knew that nobody would want to go, and he listened in despair.

Suddenly there was a dreadful noise from the cellar

below the dining room, where the cow was. The poor animal couldn't understand what was happening, and, opening its great mouth, it let out an enormous bellow of rage.

Too-Sly dropped his knife and fork in a fright, and turned pale.

'Whatever's that?' he asked.

'Oh, don't worry about that little noise,' said Mr Woff, calmly. 'That's only my dragon.'

'Your *dragon*!' said Too-Sly, in amazement. 'What do you mean – your dragon? I never heard of anyone keeping a dragon before.'

'Haven't you?' said Mr Woff, raising his eyebrows in surprise. 'Well, you see, Your Excellency, I prefer to ride on a dragon, rather than on a horse, so I captured a fine dragon last week, and put him in my cellar. He makes a good steed, I can assure you!'

The cow bellowed again. The enchanter didn't like it at all. He went on with his dinner, and he kept looking in surprise at Mr Woff. Who would have thought that such a quiet little man would be able to capture a dragon and keep him for a horse? Too-Sly was most astonished. He jumped every time the cow bellowed.

'I hope your dragon is safely tied up,' he said at last.

'Oh, I think so,' said Mr Woff. 'Let me see – *did* I tie him up, my dear Twinkle?'

'Well, if you didn't, I did,' said Twinkle. 'I hope he doesn't escape, though, Mr Woff – you know he ate two enchanters a month ago. It would be very awkward for His Excellency, Too-Sly.'

Too-Sly really felt more nervous than ever. And when the pig in the nearby pantry began to root about in the straw and grunt for all he was worth, he choked with fright and went as white as a sheet.

Mr Woff banged him on the back. 'Don't worry about *that* little noise!' he said.

'But whatever is it?' asked Too-Sly, listening to the pig's loud grunts.

'I think it must be the wizard I've got prisoner,'

said Mr Woff, listening. 'When he goes to sleep he snores terribly. Really, I shall have to make him stop sleeping.'

'What? Have you got a wizard here as a prisoner?' cried Too-Sly, putting down his spoon in amazement. 'What next! A dragon for a horse – and a wizard kept prisoner!'

'Well, Your Excellency,' said Mr Woff, helping himself to another piece of pie, 'the wizard annoyed me, you know. He *would* take the villagers for his servants, and they didn't like it. So I walked over to his house, put a spell on him, threw him over my back, brought him home here, and locked him up. I shall let him go if he promises to be good. If not, I shall give him to my dragon for dinner.'

Too-Sly stared at Mr Woff as if he couldn't believe his eyes! He felt very nervous indeed of this quiet little man. Good gracious! To think of Mr Woff throwing a wizard over his back and carrying him home! To think of him giving his dragon the wizard for dinner! Too-Sly's hands began to shake with fright. He wondered whatever Mr Woff would do to *him* if he didn't like him?

Then there came the most terrible noise from the kitchen, as Jinks dropped the twenty tin trays in a heap from the top of the kitchen steps. You should have heard it! It made even Mr Woff jump, and he, of course, was expecting the noise.

Poor Too-Sly leapt right out of his chair and fell over, bump! He sat on the floor, very pale, looking at Mr Woff in alarm.

'W-w-w-w-what's that?' he whispered, looking towards the kitchen. Mr Woff pulled him up and patted him gently on the shoulder.

'Don't be frightened,' he said. 'That's only my servant giant. Whenever he moves, his chains rattle, and that was the noise you heard.'

'What! Have you a giant for a servant?' cried the enchanter, hardly able to believe his ears.

'Why not?' said Mr Woff, taking a large helping of

ice cream. 'A giant is strong and can do much more work than an ordinary servant. I have to keep him chained, of course, or he might get loose and harm the villagers.'

At that moment the cow bellowed again and the pig grunted loudly. Too-Sly began to wish he had never come to Mr Woff's house.

Crash – bang – crash! In the kitchen Jinks let fall all the tin trays again, and Too-Sly once again leapt out of his chair, his spoonful of ice cream flying across the table.

'Pray don't be so nervous,' said Mr Woff, patting him. 'Surely you don't mind the rattle of my giant's chains! I will go and take them off him, if you like, and then you won't hear them rattling any more.'

Mr Woff got up and walked towards the kitchen door – but that was more than the enchanter could bear. He cried out in terror:

'Mr Woff! Mr Woff! No, no, do not take off your giant's chains! He might escape and do great harm.'

'Well – he certainly might eat you, Too-Sly, if he came in here and saw you,' said Mr Woff, stopping. 'I've just remembered that he hates enchanters, because one turned his mother into a frog. So perhaps he'd better keep his chains on.'

Crash – bang – crash! Once again Jinks dropped the twenty trays and once again the poor enchanter sprang out of his chair in a fearful fright.

'Perhaps you'd rather I didn't ask my servant to come and clear away the supper things?' asked Mr Woff. 'He might scare you.'

Too-Sly was in a dreadful fright to think of the giant coming into the room.

'P-p-p-p-please don't b-b-bother to have the meal cleared,' he stammered.

'Well, let's go into the study and talk about your castle,' said Mr Woff. He led the way and Too-Sly followed, wondering fearfully if this dreadful man, Mr Woff, kept any strange creatures in his study! Too-Sly wished he had never, never thought of coming to live in the village of Trim. He didn't like to think of living near a man like Mr Woff, who thought nothing of catching dragons, capturing wizards or keeping giants for servants! He had quite changed his mind about wanting to build his castle on the hill nearby – but how could he get out of it now? He thought it would be very difficult indeed.

They sat down in the little study. There were many papers on the table and Mr Woff turned them over.

'Let me see,' he said. 'I think you wanted to buy my hill, didn't you? You want to build a castle there?'

'Well – I haven't *quite* made up my mind,' said the enchanter, staring at Mr Woff.

'But dear me!' cried Mr Woff, pretending to be quite indignant, 'you can't change your mind like this, Your Excellency! Why, I've all the papers ready! What has made you alter your mind?'

'I'm not quite sure that the air will suit me here,' said Too-Sly.

'But it's very good air!' said Mr Woff, making up

his mind to make the enchanter feel as uncomfortable as possible.

'Well – I'm really very sorry to have put you to so much trouble,' said Too-Sly, 'but I don't think I can live in your village after all.'

Crash – crash – bang – bang! The trays dropped on to the kitchen floor again and the enchanter turned pale. He spoke to Mr Woff again, very hurriedly.

'But as you have gone to a lot of trouble for me today, I am quite willing to pay you one hundred gold pieces,' said he. 'That's if you'll let me off my promise to buy your hill.'

'Dear dear, this is a strange thing,' said Mr Woff, looking very sternly at Too-Sly, and enjoying himself very much indeed. 'Well, I am a reasonable man, and I agree. Pay me the hundred gold pieces, go out of my house and never come back again to my village of Trim. If you do, I will set free my dragon, I will tell the wizard to put a spell upon you, and I will send my giant to catch you! Perhaps it is just as well,

Too-Sly, that, for your own sake, you are not coming to live here!'

The cow bellowed once more in the cellar, the pig grunted loudly and the trays crashed again on the stone floor of the kitchen. Too-Sly, very pale, thought it *was* just as well that he wasn't coming to live in Trim Village. He hastily counted out one hundred gold pieces on to the study table, said goodbye to Mr Woff, and ran out of the house to his carriage as quickly as he could, his cloak flying out behind him.

The carriage door banged. The horses started off at a gallop. In half a minute the carriage was out of sight. Then Mr Woff sat down in a chair and began to laugh. Twinkle came in and began to laugh too. Jinks came in with his trays and roared when Mr Woff told him the whole story. You couldn't even hear the cow bellow or the pig grunt for the laughing of the three in the study!

'Well, I've never told so many naughty stories in my life,' said Mr Woff, wiping the tears from his eyes.

'But if you're dealing with a wily and deceitful person, he can't complain if you borrow his habits for a short while! Look at all this gold, Jinks! We'll give a most enormous party tomorrow, and invite the whole of the village to it. That will be a fine way of spending the money! Ho ho ho!'

'Ho ho ho!' laughed the others, and it was a long time before they could stop.

And what about Too-Sly, the enchanter? Well, he galloped to the other end of the kingdom and didn't stop till he got there – and certainly he never, never again visited the pretty little village of Trim!

Buttercup Magic

Buttercup Magic

CHIPPY WAS a gnome who helped old Mother Grumps with her farm-work. He ran here and there for her, milked the cows, made the butter, and groomed the horses. He was a very hard-working gnome, and Mother Grumps had no fault to find with him.

But she could not for the life of her think where all her butter went to. Such a lot was made, and put aside to sell, and yet when the time came to sell it there never seemed to be the right amount.

'Where can it go to?' asked Mother Grumps. 'Do *you* take any, husband?'

'Not I,' said her husband. 'I don't like butter enough to take any, as you know.'

'Well, do you take any?' she asked her son. But he laughed and shook his head.

'Why, mother, I would never take butter at all if you didn't make me,' he said. 'Nasty, greasy stuff!'

Then Mother Grumps went to Sally Lingumbob, her old, old nanny, and shouted in her ear:

'Do you touch any of the butter set out in the dairy, Sally?'

But Sally shook her head from side to side indignantly.

'Don't I sit up here in my room all day long?' she asked. 'How could my poor old legs take me down to the dairy and back again without you helping me?'

Well, Mother Grumps knew that was true, and she was more puzzled than ever. She really didn't know what to think.

'You ask that little gnome,' said old Sally, who had never liked Chippy. 'I expect *he* could tell you where it goes to!'

'Dear me, I'd forgotten Chippy,' said Mother

Grumps. 'But I don't think it *can* be the gnome, Sally, for he never takes butter at any meal, you know. He even has his bread dry.'

'Well, you ask him, that's all,' said Sally.

So Mother Grumps asked him.

'I can't think what happens to the butter, Chippy,' she said. 'Do you ever go into the dairy and take any?'

'Never, madam,' said Chippy. 'I don't like butter at all. Why, as you know, I never have it on my bread when I sit in the kitchen at tea with you every day.'

'No, you don't. That's quite true,' said Mother Grumps. 'Well, well, well! This is a most extraordinary thing. Here's a household that doesn't like butter, and yet it disappears steadily.'

The butter still went on vanishing, and at last Mother Grumps went to see an old friend of hers, a wise woman who lived on Blowaway Hill. She told her about her puzzle, and the wise woman laughed.

'Why, my dear,' she said, 'I will soon find out for you. I'll come along tomorrow and solve the mystery.'

So the next day she came trotting along over the buttercup fields, her skirts all yellow with pollen. Before she reached Mother Grumps's farm, she stooped and picked a fine large buttercup.

With this in her hand she knocked at Mother Grumps's door.

'Come in, come in,' cried Mother Grumps, opening the door wide. 'I'm so pleased to see you. What have you brought that buttercup for, my dear?'

'Let me hold it under your chin for a moment,' said the wise woman. Mother Grumps held up her chin, and the old woman held the buttercup underneath.

'Now it's your turn,' she said to Farmer Grumps, and she held it under *his* chin.

Then the son had to have it held under his chin too, and he said the buttercup tickled him dreadfully.

'Nonsense!' laughed the wise woman. 'Now where's old Sally Lingumbob, my dear?'

'Upstairs,' said Mother Grumps, and up they went to Sally's room. She had to have the buttercup held under *her* chin too, and she grumbled about it, and said it made her neck ache to hold her head up like that, all for a whim of the wise woman's. Why couldn't she use her buttercups on her own folk, instead of coming worrying Mother Grumps's family?

The wise woman laughed, and made no answer. 'Is there anyone else in your house?' she asked.

'Yes,' said Mother Grumps, 'there's Chippy the gnome.'

'I'll try him too with my buttercup,' said the wise woman, and she went to where the gnome was sweeping out the scullery.

He lifted up his head in surprise when she told him to, and she held the golden buttercup underneath his chin. Then she thanked him and went into the living room with Mother Grumps and shut the door.

'Chippy takes your butter,' she said gravely. 'He is very, very, very fond of it.'

'Oh, nonsense!' said Mother Grumps. 'Why, he won't even have it on his bread at tea-time.'

'That's only to make you think he doesn't like it,' said the wise woman. 'I expect he goes straight home afterwards and eats a whole lot. I tell you he loves it. Watch your dairy tonight and see if anyone gets into it.'

So that night Farmer Grumps watched his dairy, for there was a great deal of butter there, all waiting to go to market to be sold. And sure enough, at midnight, when everything was dark and silent, the dairy window slid up and someone slipped in, and ran softly over to the pile of butter.

'*Hoy!*' shouted Farmer Grumps, and jumped up from the chair in which he had been sitting half asleep. 'I've got you!'

He caught hold of someone's shoulder, and called loudly for his son to come and light a candle. Mother Grumps and her son came running along in their dressing-gowns, and soon a candle was lighted, and everyone looked to see who the thief was.

And it was Chippy, the gnome who vowed he

never took butter, because he couldn't bear it! There he stood, trembling, his hands smeared with butter, and a large slice of bread spread with butter half an inch thick!

'Oho!' cried Mother Grumps angrily. 'So it's you, is it, Chippy, you naughty little gnome! Well, you shall just have to go away and never come back again.'

Then Chippy went down on his knees and begged for forgiveness.

'I'll always be good now,' he wept. 'Please take me back, master and mistress. I'll never take butter again. But, oh, how did you find out it was I who took it?'

'How *did* the wise woman find out?' asked Farmer Grumps.

Mother Grumps shook her head. She hadn't thought to ask. But she made up her mind to find out the next day.

She went to Blowaway Hill and told the wise woman what had happened. 'But, my dear, how did you find out it was Chippy?' she asked.

'Oh, that's easy!' said the wise woman. 'Didn't you know that buttercups once had a butter spell put on them? Whenever you hold them under anyone's chin, you can find out if that person likes butter, for you will see a golden light come under their chin, just the colour of new-made butter. As soon as I popped the buttercup under Chippy's chin I knew he was the thief, for the golden light almost dazzled me! So I knew he was very, very fond of butter!'

'Well, you were quite right,' said Mother Grumps. 'But, dear me, fancy buttercups being magic enough to tell you all that! I really must tell my friends!'

'No, don't do that,' said the wise woman. 'I want it to be kept secret.'

But Mother Grumps simply *couldn't* keep a secret, and soon all her village knew about the buttercups. Then the next village got to know, and the next, and the next. And now there isn't a place in the kingdom that doesn't know that buttercups will tell you if you like butter.

You know it, of course, don't you? – but if you don't, be sure to pick a fine large buttercup this June and hold it under your sister's chin, or your brother's. Say, 'Do you like butter?' and you will see the answer underneath their chin, as clear as can be – for a lovely golden light will shine there, as yellow as new-made butter!

The Wizard's
Pink Cloak

The Wizard's Pink Cloak

HEY-PRESTO THE wizard had a wonderful cloak. Whenever he swung it round his shoulders he disappeared at once, because it had very powerful magic in it.

The cloak was most useful to the wizard. He wore it whenever he wanted to be invisible, and then he was able to do all kinds of things.

He could slip into other wizards' castles and watch them at their magic work without being seen. He could go into witch Green-Eyes' cottage and stand unseen beside her as she stirred spells into her big black pot. He could swing his cloak round him when visitors came that he didn't want to bother about. Nobody could see him then!

'A most useful cloak!' said Hey-Presto, whenever he hung it up in his cupboard and locked the door. 'An invaluable cloak! I couldn't do without it. I must never, never let my enemies get it.'

One day when he took it out of the cupboard, Miggy, his old servant, saw it.

'Good gracious, Master!' she said. 'How can you wear that dirty old cloak? What colour is it meant to be? It's so dirty that I can't even tell if it's blue, red or green!'

'It's pink,' said the wizard, looking at it. 'At least, it's supposed to be pink! It does look dirty, doesn't it? Well, well – I suppose I've used it for over a hundred years now – no wonder it is dirty!'

'It's smelly, too,' said Miggy, wrinkling her nose. 'Pooh! It needs washing, Master. Fancy using a thing for over a hundred years and not having it washed. And look at this hole!'

'Dear me, yes,' said the wizard, quite alarmed. 'It won't do to get big holes in it – bits of me will be seen then, through the holes. Whatever shall I do?'

'I'll wash and mend it,' said Miggy, firmly.

'It's too precious,' said Hey-Presto, clutching it tightly.

'Now listen,' said Miggy. 'That cloak smells so dirty that very soon people will know you are near them, even though you're invisible. You let me wash it. I'll be very, very careful.'

'All right, Miggy. But when you hang it out to dry, please put up a clothes-line in the walled garden and make sure the gate is locked,' said Hey-Presto. 'If anyone saw this cloak on the line they might steal it!'

'Oh, Master, I'll be as careful of your cloak as if it were made of gold!' said old Miggy, putting it over her arm. 'My word – what a horrible smell! It must be five hundred years old, not one!'

She went off and got a tub full of boiling water. In

went the magic cloak, and Miggy scrubbed it up and down in the suds.

'Just look at the dirt coming out,' said Miggy, in disgust. 'Why, there's more dirt than cloak! I'll have to wash it three or four times before it's really clean.'

When she had finished washing it, she could hardly believe her eyes! The cloak was pink – the loveliest pink imaginable!

Miggy shook it out and then called her master. 'Master, come here! Did you ever see such a lovely colour in your life?'

Hey-Presto looked at his cloak. Why, it didn't seem the same one! 'It's the colour of almond blossom!' he said. 'It's the colour of wild roses in the hedge! And yes – it's exactly the colour of the sky when it's pink at sunset time!'

'Yes,' said Miggy. 'Shame on you for wearing it so dirty! I'm going to hang it out to dry and then I'll mend it for you.'

'In the walled garden, mind!' called the wizard, anxiously. 'Nobody can get in there, nobody at all.'

Miggy hurried into the walled garden. She had already put up a washing-line there. She went to the door in the wall and locked it carefully, putting the key into her pocket. Now nobody could get into the garden from outside, and the walls were far too high to climb.

She looked at the clouds racing across the sky. *Nice windy day – the cloak will dry quickly!* she thought. *I'll press it tonight and mend it – and I'll see that the master doesn't get it so dirty again. It shan't go for more than twenty years this time before it's washed again.*

She pegged the cloak carefully on the line and watched it flapping in the wind. It would soon be dry!

I'll fetch it about three o'clock, she thought and trotted indoors. She kept an eye on it through the kitchen window, and was pleased to see that it was drying nicely.

At three o'clock she went into the garden to unpeg

the cloak – but it wasn't there! The line was empty – and three or four clothes pegs lay scattered on the ground!

Miggy gave a scream that brought Hey-Presto out at once. 'Master! *Master!* Your cloak's been stolen!'

Hey-Presto came at top speed. He saw the empty washing-line and the scattered pegs and he groaned. He ran to the garden door that led out into the lane, but it was locked. No one could have got in that way.

'I kept that cloak under my eye the whole time,' sobbed Miggy. 'I looked out from the kitchen window almost every minute. Nobody could have got in without my seeing them, nobody! They couldn't get out without being seen either.'

'Oh, yes they could,' said Hey-Presto, grimly. 'All the thief had to do was to swing the cloak round his shoulders and he and the cloak too would be invisible at once. He could go where he liked then – even creep in past you through the kitchen, out into the hall and walk out of the front door. Nobody would see him. What am I to do? My wonderful cloak! I must get it back!'

'The thief won't always be wearing it, sir, and it's such a bright, glowing pink that it would be very easy to recognise it,' said poor Miggy, very upset indeed. 'Can't you offer a reward, Master, to anyone – even to any animal or bird – who finds it or brings news of it?'

'Yes. Yes, I'll certainly do that,' said Hey-Presto. Immediately he sent out hundreds of little pixie heralds, complete with trumpets, to announce his loss and the reward for finding the cloak.

Everyone was excited. The country was searched from top to bottom. But no news came in. Nobody had ever seen the cloak, hardly anyone had even known of it – so how could it have been stolen?

Rabbits searched down burrows. Fish in the rivers hunted here and there. Owls looked in hollow trees, swallows looked in barns. It was no good – nobody saw anything pink that was big enough to be the cloak.

And then one day a chaffinch flew down to Miggy in great excitement. 'Pink!' he called loudly. 'Pink-pink!'

'What do you mean? Have you found the pink cloak?' cried Miggy. 'Where is it?'

'Pink-pink-pink!' shouted the little chaffinch, fluffing out his pretty chest. 'PINK!'

'I'll come with you,' said Miggy, putting on her bonnet. 'Lead the way, Chaffinch. I'm sure you think you've found the cloak!'

'Chip-chip-chip-chip, cherry-erry-erry, chippy, here-we-are!' sang the chaffinch, flying up into a tall tree just outside the walled garden. And there, caught on a high branch, and wrapped round and round it, was the magic cloak, as pink as ever, but a little dirty.

'Yes! You're right! It is the cloak!' cried Miggy. 'You clever bird, you very clever bird! Wait here till I get a ladder, and don't you dare to tell anyone else!'

She fetched a long ladder and up and up she went.

She unwrapped the cloak from the branch and slipped it round her so that she might use both her hands to climb down the ladder again. At once, to the chaffinch's astonishment, she vanished and the cloak vanished, too!

'Pink!' he called anxiously. Miggy's voice answered him from the ladder.

'It's all right. I'm still here, climbing down the ladder. Wearing the cloak is the easiest way for me to carry it!'

She ran to the wizard, taking the cloak off just as she got to him. 'Master! It's found! Here it is!'

'Where was it?' asked Hey-Presto, startled and delighted.

'Caught up in a tree not far from the walled garden!' said Miggy. 'Nobody stole it! The strong wind must have blown it off the line straight up into the tree and wrapped it round a branch – and there it's been ever since!'

'But who found it?' asked Hey-Presto, looking to

see if the cloak was damaged.

'The chaffinch who nests in that tree,' said Miggy. 'He came and told me. He was so excited he could only say, "Pink! Pink!" But I guessed what he meant, of course.'

'Then he must have the reward,' said Hey-Presto. 'Call him here, the clever bird.'

The chaffinch came. He flew in at the window, calling, 'Pink! Pink!'

'There! He can't say anything but that at the moment,' said Miggy. 'He's been shouting out the news to everyone – he's so proud of himself!'

'Chaffinch, you have earned the reward,' said Hey-Presto, and the little bird flew on to his shoulder. 'You may have a sack of gold – a box of spells – or anything else you can think of.'

The chaffinch whispered a little song into the wizard's ear. Hey-Presto laughed.

'What does he want for a reward?' asked Miggy.

'Nothing! He says money is no use to him – and

he's frightened of spells – and as he has a nest of his own, with a dear little wife and four beautiful nestlings. He has got everything he can possibly want,' said the wizard. 'He just wants to know if he can go on telling everyone that he found my pink cloak – he's so very, very proud of that.'

'Well, let him,' said Miggy. 'It's a reward that won't cost you a penny – and he'll be glad that he and all his family can boast about finding your magic cloak. People love boasting – even birds do!'

'You're right,' said Hey-Presto, and he turned to the excited little chaffinch. He spoke very solemnly.

'As your reward for finding my pink cloak you may tell everyone in the world!' he said. 'You may shout the news at the top of your voice year after year!'

And, believe it or not, from that day to this every chaffinch shouts out the news each spring and summer. You must listen, you really must.

'Pink!' he calls loudly. 'Pink, pink, pink!'

Listen for him, will you, and call out, 'Clever bird!

Who found the magic cloak? What colour was it?'

And he will put his knowing little head on one side and answer you at once.

'Pink! Pink-pink-pink!'

The Dog that Helped a Fairy

The Dog that Helped a Fairy

BOBS WAS a jolly little fox-terrier dog. He lived with Benny, his small master, and they had fine games together. Benny taught Bobs to sit up and beg, and to balance a biscuit on his nose. When Benny said, 'Paid for!' Bobs would toss his nose up, throw the biscuit into the air and catch it, very cleverly, in his mouth.

The two often went for long walks together. They were very fond of one another, and when Benny was naughty and had been told off, Bobs would sit close to him and put his nose into Benny's hands. That was very comforting to Benny.

'I do wish you could talk, Bobs!' Benny would

often say. 'If only you could, how fine it would be! We should be able to be even greater friends then, because you could tell me all your thoughts and secrets, just as I tell you mine!'

But Bobs couldn't talk. He could whine, yelp, growl, wuff and bark, but he couldn't say a word. He often wished he could, for there were many things he would have loved to tell Benny.

One day Benny and Bobs went for a walk in Sandy Woods. Bobs loved that walk because there were so many rabbits about. It was most exciting to poke his nose down all the holes and smell rabbit, rabbit, rabbit!

Benny was looking for birds' nests. He never took any eggs, but he loved to see the sky-blue of the hedge-sparrows' eggs, or the pretty brown-red eggs of the robins. Bobs ran on in front. He knew of a fine rabbit hole not far off, and he meant to have a good sniff down it!

On he ran, leaving Benny behind him – and

suddenly he heard a most peculiar noise! It sounded like a parrot-screech, and after that came a sound of weeping. Bobs pricked up his silky black ears; then he ran quickly towards the strange sounds.

And, dear me, he saw a strange sight! A green-eyed witch was dragging a small fairy along by the wings! Bobs could hardly believe his eyes. Benny had often told him about fairies and witches and giants, but he had never in his little doggy life seen any before. And now here were two!

The witch was making the parrot-like screeching noises. She was quite delighted because she had caught a fairy.

The frightened little prisoner was weeping loudly. 'Let me go! Let me go! You'll break my wings!'

'You shall come and be my servant and sweep and scrub my house for me!' screeched the green-eyed witch. 'I have wanted a servant like you for a long time.'

Then the small fairy caught sight of the surprised

dog peeping between the trees, and she called to him. 'Help! Help! Little dog, come and save me!'

The witch looked round and saw Bobs. She glared at him and cried, 'If you come near me I'll turn you into a bone!'

Bobs was frightened. He didn't at all want to be turned into a bone. Why, he might be eaten by another dog, then! But the poor little fairy's crying nearly broke his kind little heart. He really must help her!

So he rushed up to the angry witch and – would you believe it – he bit her on the leg! She gave a loud squawk, dropped the little fairy and hopped round and round, holding her leg, and shouting, 'I'll turn you into a bone, yes, I will, I'll turn you into a bone!'

'Quickly!' whispered the fairy into Bobs's ear. 'Run away with me before she remembers the spell to turn you into a bone!'

'Jump on my back!' wuffed Bobs, and the fairy understood his barks quite well. She slipped softly on to his hairy back, and off he galloped at top speed.

The old witch saw him and cried out a string of strange, very magic words. It was the spell to change Bobs into a bone!

But he was out of sight before the spell could work properly, and how glad he was! Still, something strange seemed to have happened to his tail. He couldn't move it. Whatever was the matter with it? It wouldn't wag properly.

'Oh dear, your poor tail has changed into a bone!' said the fairy suddenly. 'A bit of the spell must have acted after all. What a good thing we got away when we did!'

'Wuff, wuff!' said Bobs, sadly, looking at his strange bone-tail. Whatever would Benny say when he saw it? What would other dogs say? Bobs felt very unhappy.

The fairy saw his ears drooping sadly, and she slipped off his back and hugged him. 'Don't look so miserable,' she said. 'Cheer up! Come along to Pixieland with me, and I'll get my aunt, Dame

Tweedles, to put your tail right again!'

She took hold of Bobs's collar and led him to a very big rabbit-hole, the biggest that Bobs had ever seen. And just as he was about to go down it, what should he hear but Benny's whistle! Then he heard Benny calling him.

'Bobs! Bobs! Where are you?'

'Quick! Come with me, or you'll never get your tail right!' said the fairy, pulling him down the hole. 'I'll take you back to Benny afterwards.'

So Bobs disappeared down the very large rabbit hole with the fairy, wondering what Benny would think when he didn't go running to him as usual.

Now, Benny just happened to come down the path as Bobs was disappearing down the hole. He was most astonished to see Bobs running down a rabbit hole instead of coming when he was called. He stood and stared, wondering if Bobs would come back – but he didn't.

'Well, how strange!' said Benny. He bent down and looked into the hole – and then he saw a most surprising thing! Not far down that dark hole was a lamp, shining brightly! Whoever heard of a lamp hung in a rabbit hole? Benny never had, and he guessed at once that it was not a real rabbit hole. There must be something magic about it!

He bent down and looked into it. It was a very big hole. It was really big enough for him to get down it, with a squeeze. He wondered if he should.

Then, far down the hole, he heard a little bark.

'That's Bobs!' he said. 'Why didn't he come when I whistled to him? I wonder whether some witch has got hold of him. Oh dear! I must go down and see. I should have to save him if he was in danger.'

So down that big hole Benny squeezed himself. Soon he came to the lamp – and then he saw that the hole widened out into a passage set with shallow steps that went down and down.

This is a real adventure! thought the little boy, going

down the steps. He went down about a hundred and then he came to a low, stout door set across the passage. A lamp shone over it, and on the door was printed one word in big letters: PUSH.

So Benny pushed and the door swung open. To the little boy's enormous surprise he was looking out on a sunshiny village, whose pretty little cottages had thatched roofs and windows set with small diamond-panes.

'Well, who would have thought that such a place could be down at the bottom of a big rabbit hole!' thought Benny in surprise. He stepped through the door, and looked round. There were many small fairies, pixies and gnomes going about their business, some with shopping baskets, some with bags. They didn't seem at all surprised to see Benny.

'Please, have you seen a small fox-terrier dog?' asked Benny, stopping a pointy-eared pixie.

'Yes, it went down that way,' said the little creature, pointing down the village street. Benny went on, looking everywhere for Bobs. But he couldn't see him.

So he asked a gnome, and the gnome said, yes, he had seen a dog going to Hollyhock Cottage, not far down the lane. So off went Benny again.

Very soon he came to Hollyhock Cottage. He knew it must be, because although there was no name on the gate, great red and pink hollyhocks grew all round the walls.

Benny stopped and listened – yes, he could quite well hear little wuffs and barks from inside the cottage. Bobs must be there!

He whistled loudly and waited. No Bobs came. He whistled again. Still no Bobs, but once more he heard the wuffs and barks. Bobs must be inside, and someone must be keeping him prisoner, or surely he would come running out to Benny!

The little boy crept round to the back of the cottage. There was a window there and he peeped in. What a strange sight he saw!

Bobs was standing in the middle of a ring of white

chalk. Benny stared at his dog's tail, for it was just like a long butcher's bone! Benny suddenly felt angry! Were they doing some horrid magic to his dear little dog? How had his nice tail got like that?

He saw a little fairy stroking Bobs's head, and on the other side of the chalk ring stood an old dame, a bright red shawl wrapped round her shoulders. She was chanting a song made of strange words. Benny knew they were magic.

'I must rescue Bobs!' he thought. 'Surely they are weaving a spell over him, and he will be turned into something horrid. Bobs, Bobs!'

Calling his dog loudly he flung open the window and jumped inside. The fairy screamed and the old woman stared in astonishment. Bobs stood quite still for he was under a spell and couldn't move.

'Don't go into the magic ring!' begged the fairy, hanging on to Benny's arm. 'Please don't! If you do you'll spoil the magic, and we shan't be able to make your dog's tail right again.'

'Oh,' said Benny, stopping. 'Are you trying to help him, then? I thought you were working a horrid spell on him.'

'Of course not!' said the old dame, indignantly. 'We are trying to make his bone-tail disappear and his own tail grow again. Watch now, and keep quiet.'

So Benny watched, and as he stood there and looked, he saw Bobs's curious bone-tail gradually fade away into a sort of mist. For a minute the little dog stood in the ring with no tail at all – and then, to Benny's delight, his own hairy tail began to grow, and at last it was all there – and all of a sudden it began to wag!

Bobs leapt out of the magic ring and jumped up at Benny in joy. 'Wuff, wuff, wuff!' he barked.

'How did you get here, and what has happened, Bobs?' asked Benny, patting the excited little dog.

'Wuff, wuff, wuff!' barked Bobs.

'Oh, I do wish you could tell me how you got here and why!' said Benny.

'Can't you understand what he is saying?' asked the fairy in surprise. 'I can understand his wuffs and barks quite plainly.'

'Well, I can't!' said Benny. 'I've often wished I could. That's the only thing that comes between Bobs and me – he can understand all I say, but I never know what he is barking.'

'Bobs,' said the fairy, turning to the little dog who at once licked her small hand. 'Bobs, I want to give you a reward for helping me to get away from that horrid green-eyed witch. Listen now – would you like me to give you a proper voice, like Benny's?'

'Wuff, wuff!' barked Bobs, jumping round everyone in great delight.

'Bobs says he would like to be able to talk to you,' said the fairy, beaming at Benny. 'Would you really like him to? You would be able to talk to each other as much as you liked, whenever you liked.'

'Oh, yes, I'd like that more than anything else in the world!' said Benny at once, his heart beating in excitement.

'Very well,' said the fairy. 'Aunt Tweedles, would you give me a talking spell, please?'

The old dame went to a drawer and opened it. She took out a round box and slid off the lid. Inside were a great many little blue pills. She took one out and gave it to Benny.

'Give this to your dog before he goes to sleep tonight,' she said. 'Then in the morning he will be able to talk as you do. But remember this – he must only talk to you. If he tries to talk to anyone else his voice will go and never come back!'

Benny took the pill and thanked the old dame and the fairy very much.

Then he and Bobs went to the strange tunnel and made their way back to the wood. They were both so excited that they could hardly go fast enough!

That night Benny gave Bobs the pill and the little dog swallowed it whole. He wuffed, but didn't say a word. His voice hadn't yet grown!

But the next morning when Benny went to see him, what a wonderful surprise!

'Good morning, Benny!' said a gruff doggy voice. 'I can talk! I can talk! And first let me say something I've always wanted to say to you.'

'What is that?' asked Benny, delighted.

'I love you, little master, and I think you are the finest person in the world!' said Bobs, jumping up to lick Benny's ear.

Well, wasn't that a lovely thing to hear from his dog? Benny was so pleased that he didn't know what to say. But very soon the two were chattering nineteen to the dozen, which means that they both talked at once, without stopping, for a very long time!

I know Bobs quite well – but I've never asked him to talk to me. It would be such a pity if he lost his funny, doggy voice, wouldn't it! So if ever you meet him, don't try and make him talk, will you?

The Page that
Blew Away

The Page that
Blew Away

OLD DAME Candy kept a fine little shop. It was a sweet-shop, and my goodness me, you should have seen the sweets she had in it!

It was no wonder the pixies and brownies pressed their noses against the window all day long, pointing to this and that.

'Oooh – butter-nut toffee,' said one.

'And honey-balls,' said another.

'And peppermint rock and raspberry drops and sugar-marbles!' said someone else. 'How does Dame Candy think of all these lovely sweets?'

'She has a magic book,' said Snoopy. 'I've seen it.'

'So have I,' said Pry.

Both pixies nodded their heads. Yes – they had seen Dame Candy's book.

'Have you read it?' asked one of the brownies looking into the shop.

'Oh, no – we've only seen it from a distance,' said Snoopy. 'We live next door to Dame Candy, you know, and one day we put our heads out of the window and there she was, reading her magic sweet-book in the garden.'

'We saw her making her sweets from the spells in her book,' said Pry. 'We did really.'

'Piles of sugar-marbles, dozens of toffee-delights, hundreds of candy kisses,' said Snoopy. 'She just stirred something in a jug and muttered some magic words – then she tipped up the jug and out came lots of sweets. She poured them into a dish.'

'And sold them in her shop next day,' said Pry. 'My, wouldn't I like to get hold of that book!'

They had never been able to do that because

Dame Candy kept the book under the rug in her cat's basket. Her cat always slept there, night and day, and if she wasn't there, the dog got in to keep the basket warm. So Snoopy and Pry never had a chance to borrow the book.

But one day something unexpected happened. Pry saw Dame Candy sitting out at her garden table with her jug, dish and magic book. Aha! She was going to make a new batch of wonderful sweets. He called Snoopy.

'Look – she's making sweets again, using the spells in her magic book,' whispered Pry. 'If only she would leave her garden for a minute, we might be able to slip over the wall and have a look at the book.'

'She'd turn us into toffee-balls if she saw us,' said Snoopy. 'And sell us, too!'

'Yes – we won't do anything silly,' said Pry, with a shiver.

They watched from the window. Dame Candy had already poured a heap of brown chocolates from her jug, and each chocolate had half a cherry on it. They did look nice.

And then one of the chocolates rolled off the table on to the grass. Dame Candy bent down to pick it up. At that very moment the wind blew hard – and a loose page in the magic book flew up into the air! It flew over the wall into Snoopy's garden, and settled down under a bush. Snoopy clutched Pry.

'Did you see?' he whispered. 'A page flew out of the magic book – and it's in our garden!'

'Shh!' said Pry.

Dame Candy was coming to the wall. 'Snoopy! Pry!' she called. 'A page from my book has flown into your garden. Please get it for me.'

'Come down and pretend to look everywhere,' said Snoopy to Pry. 'When you get a chance, put the page into your pocket. Then we'll say we can't find it and ask her in to look if she likes.'

'Good! We'll read the page and make sweets all for ourselves!' said Pry. Down into the garden they went.

Dame Candy had gone back to her seat. Pry put his head over the wall.

'We're just going to look for your page, Dame Candy,' he called. 'We'll hand it to you as soon as we've got it.'

'Very well,' said Dame Candy. 'Look hard.'

It didn't take Pry long to stuff the page into his pocket. Then Snoopy called over the wall.

'So sorry, Dame Candy, but we can't find the page anywhere. Would you like to come over and look?'

'No, thank you. I'm busy,' said Dame Candy. 'But let me warn you, Snoopy and Pry – if you keep the page yourself, and try to make sweets, I shall know it. Oh, yes, I shall know it!'

'We shouldn't dream of doing such a thing,' said Snoopy, with a grin at Pry. The two went indoors, chuckling.

'That was easy as winking,' said Pry. 'Now let's see what the page is about.'

They shut the windows and drew the curtains.

They didn't want anyone peeping in! Then they looked at the page out of Dame Candy's magic book.

'It's about peppermint rock,' said Pry, in delight. 'Our favourite sweet – would you believe it! Peppermint rock!'

'We'll make heaps and heaps,' said Snoopy, rubbing his hands together. 'What does the spell say?'

'We have to have a jug and a dish,' said Pry, reading the page. 'Well, we know that already. And we have to wear something blue to do this spell. Oh – so that's why old Dame Candy always wears a blue shawl round her! Have we anything blue to wear, Snoopy?'

'Our new blue caps!' said Snoopy, and they went to put them on.

'It's a very easy spell!' said Pry. 'Look, we have to pour milk into the jug, stir with a poppyolly feather, drop in a lighted match, and then say, "Tirry-lirry-roona-moona-accra-rilly-POM!" And that's all.'

'It seems very easy indeed,' said Snoopy. 'Is that really all?'

'Well, look at the page yourself,' said Pry. So Snoopy looked. Yes, that was all.

They fetched a jug and a dish. They poured milk into the jug. They got their poppyolly feather from the cupboard, and then they lit a match and dropped it into the jug. What a fizzle-fizzle, and what a strange green flame!

'Now for the magic word,' said Pry, snatching up the page. 'I'll say it – and you can pour out the peppermint rock, Snoopy. I hope our dish is big enough!'

He said the magic word loudly and clearly. 'Tirry-lirry-roona-moona-accra-rilly-POM!'

And then Snoopy at once tipped up the jug and poured it out. He looked greedily for sticks and sticks of peppermint rock – but all that came out was a stream of fine yellow powder!

'Pooh – what's this? This isn't peppermint!' said Pry, disappointed. 'It's just powder. Something's gone wrong.'

'I'm going to sneeze,' said Snoopy, suddenly, and he

sneezed very loudly indeed. '*Whooosh-oo!*'

He sneezed all over the dish, and the yellow powder flew up into the air at once. Pry felt a sneeze coming too. He threw back his head and sneezed violently. '*Whooosh-oo, whooosh-oo, whooosh-oo!*'

Then Snoopy joined in again, and soon both pixies were sneezing without stopping. The yellow powder flew all over the place, and the more it flew, the more they sneezed.

'What's happening?' gasped Pry, at last. 'Oh, Snoopy – can this yellow powder be pepper? Have we made pepper instead of peppermint? *Whooosh-oo!*'

'We must have, *whoosh-oo!*' said Snoopy. 'The spell's gone wrong.'

There was a rap at the door. The pixies looked at one another, startled. 'Who's there?' called Pry.

'Dame Candy,' said a voice. 'I've come for the page of my magic book. I told you I should soon know if you had it. I just waited to hear you sneeze – and you did!'

'*Whooosh-oo!*' sneezed Snoopy and Pry together.

The door opened and in came Dame Candy. She saw the page on the table and took it. The pixies went on sneezing miserably.

'You only had half the peppermint spell,' said Dame Candy. 'You have to read the bit on the next page in my book to complete the spell – then you'd have got a jugful of peppermint rock instead of pepper. Serves you right!'

She went out with the page of her magic book. Pry ran to the door.

'Take the pepper, please take it,' he cried. '*Whoosh-oo!*'

'No, you can keep it,' said Dame Candy, with a laugh. 'It's all over your kitchen by now – you won't get rid of it for days. That will teach you to take things that belong to someone else, Snoopy and Pry!'

It did – and it was a dreadful lesson to learn, because Snoopy and Pry didn't stop sneezing for nine days. And now, it's such a pity, they can't bear even to look at peppermint rock. That starts them sneezing again too! They'll be careful not to meddle with Dame Candy's spells again, won't they?

Little Marya
and the Witch

Little Marya
and the Witch

ONCE UPON a time there was a little Russian girl called Marya. Her mother was dead, and her father married again, so Marya had a stepmother.

Now, this stepmother did not like Marya, because the child's father was fond of her. So she treated her badly, and made her work very hard.

They lived far away from everybody else on the edge of a great pine forest. The only person who lived at all near to them was a witch who lived in a curious little hut. This hut was perched on one leg, and spun round all day. The witch was not a nice woman, and no one went near her if they could possibly help it.

One day Marya's stepmother said to her, 'Marya, I have no buttons to put on your father's new shirt. Run to the witch and ask her to lend me some.'

Marya looked at her stepmother in surprise, for she knew that it was dangerous to go near the witch.

'Go quickly,' said her stepmother, 'or I will beat you, Marya.'

Marya did not dare to say she would not go, for she was afraid of being beaten. So she started off with some bread and bacon in a bag, weeping to herself, and wondering what the witch would say when she saw her.

On the way through the forest she met a woodman who looked at her out of kind, wise eyes.

'Why do you weep, little one?' he asked.

'Because I have been sent to the witch,' said Marya, 'and I am afraid.'

'Do not be afraid,' said the woodman. 'I will help you. Now, listen carefully to me.'

Marya listened.

'You will find dogs at the witch's house, who would eat you if they could. Throw them bread to eat and they will leave you alone. There is a cat there too, who would scratch your eyes out if it could. Give it bacon to eat, and it will purr. The door will creak, so oil it well. That is all, Marya. Remember my words, and no harm will come to you.'

Marya said thank you to the wise woodman, and went on her way again. Very soon she saw the witch's hut in the distance. It was spinning round and round on its one leg, and looked strange and mysterious. Marya wished she could go home, but she dared not return without the shirt buttons her stepmother wanted.

She went over to the hut, and as she drew near it spun more slowly, and at last stopped. Marya knocked at the door.

'Come in,' said a voice.

Marya went in. The witch was sitting at her loom, weaving.

'Good morning,' said she. Marya looked at her, and thought she had never seen such an ugly old creature before.

'I have come to borrow some buttons to sew on my father's shirt,' she said timidly.

The witch smiled strangely.

'Wait here while I get them,' she said. 'Take my place at the loom, and go on with the weaving.'

She got up, and Marya sat down in her place. The witch went out of the room and left her alone. She began to cry for she didn't know what was going to happen to her in that odd little hut.

Suddenly she heard a fierce hissing sound, and she saw that a great black cat had come into the room. It was glaring at her, and stretching its claws.

Marya remembered what the wise woodman had said. She quickly undid her little bag and pulled out the piece of bacon she had brought. She threw it to the big cat.

It began purring at once, and ate the bacon hungrily.

Then it licked its lips, and looked at Marya.

'Oh, black cat, help me to escape!' cried Marya. 'I believe the witch will keep me prisoner and make me her servant.'

'That is just what she will do,' said the cat in a deep purring voice. 'You must run off at once while there is a chance. Stop now and again and lay your ear to the ground to hear if the witch is coming. Take this towel and this comb with you, and if you hear her coming throw down first the towel, and afterwards the comb. They will help to save you.'

Marya listened, and took the towel and the comb. She thanked the cat, and tiptoed to the door. Then she remembered that the woodman had said it would creak. If it did, perhaps the witch would hear her and come in to stop her going.

She quickly looked round, and on a shelf she saw a can of oil. She took it down and hurriedly oiled the hinges of the door. Then she opened it without a sound and stepped out into a little yard.

Three great dogs were there, and began to growl when they saw her, but she emptied her bag of bread among them and they let her go. Off she ran into the forest, and was soon lost to sight.

The black cat sat down at Marya's place at the loom and began weaving. Presently the witch looked in at the window and called out, 'Are you still weaving, Marya?'

The cat pretended to be Marya and answered, 'Yes, I am weaving, dear witch!'

The witch knew at once that it was not Marya's voice and she rushed into the hut in a great rage.

'How dare you let that girl escape?'

'She was kind to me,' said the cat. 'You never gave me anything to eat, but she gave me all her bacon.'

Then the witch scolded the door for letting Marya out.

'Haven't I told you that you are only to open inwards and not outwards?' she cried.

'Marya was kind to me,' said the door. 'She gave my

poor, old, creaking hinges oil, and you never once gave me even a drop.'

Then the witch went to the dogs and scolded them well.

'Haven't I told you never to let anyone go past you!' she stormed.

'Marya was kind to us,' they said. 'You have given us no food for two days, but Marya gave us all the bread she had.'

Then the witch was very angry, and made up her mind to go after Marya and bring her back.

So off she went in her carriage, rumbling quickly along, catching up with Marya.

Marya had run through the forest on her way home, and had already gone a good distance. Suddenly she remembered what the cat had told her to do, so she stopped and put her ear to the ground to see if she could hear the witch coming.

She heard the rumbling of the carriage, and was afraid. Then lo and behold! She saw the witch in the distance, coming nearer and nearer.

Quickly she flung down the towel the cat had given her – and to her enormous surprise it turned into a wide, rushing river.

The witch soon reached it, and looked at it angrily for it was too wide and deep to cross. She saw Marya on the other side, running away as fast as ever she could.

The witch went back and got ten pairs of oxen, which she drove to the river bank. She made them drink all the water up, but it took a long time, and when at last she got across, Marya could not be seen.

The little girl was still a good way from home, though, and after a time she stopped and once more put her ear to the ground and listened. Again she could hear the witch coming nearer. So she took the comb the cat had given her and flung it on the ground.

Lo and behold! It turned into a great tangle of thornwood, so thick and so tall that no one could possibly make their way through it.

When the witch came to it, she tried to force her way into it, but the thorns held her and scratched, and she had to come out again. Once more she tried, and yet again, and all the time Marya was getting nearer and nearer home.

At last she got so near her home that she could see her stepmother baking bread in the kitchen. But she dared not go into the house, because she had not brought the shirt buttons she had been sent to get.

She sat down outside, wondering what to do, for she was afraid that the witch might come. Just at that moment the wise woodman came through the forest, and saw Marya sitting sadly outside her home.

'You have escaped from the witch then,' he said. 'That is well done. Tell me about it.'

Marya told him.

'But I dare not go home,' she said, 'because I bring no shirt buttons for my stepmother.'

The woodman's face grew stern.

'I will take you in,' he said. 'You are safe with me, little Marya.'

So he put her on his shoulders and carried her indoors. Her stepmother was most surprised to see her. Her father knew nothing of how his little daughter had been sent to the witch, and wondered why the woodman looked so stern.

Then the woodman told of the adventures which Marya had had that day, and how brave she had been. All the time he spoke he looked sternly at the stepmother, till she could bear it no longer.

'I have done wrong,' she cried. 'Forgive me, husband, and forgive me, Marya. I will be good to you now.'

And so she was, and Marya soon grew to love her stepmother, and forgot all about the old witch.

As for the witch, she got stuck so fast in the thornwood that she was never able to get out, and there she is to this very day.

Mighty-One
the Wizard

Mighty-One the Wizard

THERE ONCE lived a golden-haired princess whose name was Mirabelle. She was sweet and good, and the king and queen were proud of her. But one day she vanished from the palace, and for two whole months not a word was heard of her.

Then the North Wind, who blows into every hole and corner at some time or other, came with a message to the king.

'I have seen the Princess Mirabelle,' he said, in his blustery voice, and he blew all round the palace, making the king and queen shiver in their shoes.

'Where is she, oh where is she?' cried the king.

'She is imprisoned in the castle of Mighty-One, the wizard of Ho-Ho Land,' answered the wind, blowing the king's crown to one side. 'I saw her at the top window, and I touched her pretty golden hair and knew that she was Mirabelle. You must send a message to the wizard if you want her back.'

'Oh, thank you for telling me,' said the king. The wind bowed and flew off, setting all the curtains swaying in the wind, and blowing over a big vase of flowers.

The king called a meeting and all the nobles came to it. They discussed what must be done to rescue the poor princess, but nobody dared to offer to go to the wizard's castle. So at last the king called the North Wind back again, and told him to go to Ho-Ho Land and ask the wizard what they must do to get Princess Mirabelle back.

The wind was quite willing. He was afraid of nothing and nobody. He swept off, sending a trail of dust down the road, making everyone there sneeze and cough.

In two days the North Wind blew back again. He had been to Ho-Ho Land in a gale of a hundred miles an hour, and had spoken with the wizard Mighty-One.

'He says, O King, that you and all your court must journey to his castle. He will allow you to take Mirabelle back with you on condition that you are able to do three things.' The wind blew round the palace room, and the king drew his cloak closely round him. This North Wind was really a rough fellow.

'What are the three things?' asked the king eagerly. 'I am rich and I can buy anything in the world!'

'First, you must give the wizard something that nobody in the world has set eyes on before,' said the North Wind. 'Second, you must ask the wizard to do something he is not able to do – and I'm sure I don't know what you'll think of for that, because, O King, by his magic powers he can do almost anything in the world! And third, you must tell him what he is thinking of at the moment you stand before him!'

The king turned pale. How could he do three such difficult things? They were impossible! He might perhaps get some treasure out of the depths of the earth, a precious stone that no one had set eyes on before – but how could it be got without being seen? As for asking the wizard to do something that he couldn't do, well, that was certainly a puzzle. Thirdly, how in the world was he to know what the wizard was thinking of when he saw him? The king groaned aloud.

'Suppose I fail?' he said to the wind. 'What will happen?'

'Oh, you and all your court will become Mighty-One's servants,' the wind answered, puffing into the king's ear.

'In that case, I and my court will certainly not go,' said the king, decidedly. 'I shall not become any wizard's servant.'

But the queen thought differently. She wanted the Princess Mirabelle back again, even if it meant that all of the court, herself and the king too, fell into the wizard's power.

'Even if we do have to become his servants, we shall at least be where Mirabelle is,' she said. 'We must certainly go. But first we must think what to take with us that no one has ever set eyes on before.'

The king and queen and all the court tried in vain to think of something. The best idea they could get was to send a blind dwarf underground and bid him to search about until he found a ruby.

'As he is blind he won't see it,' said the king. 'He shall put it into a casket as soon as he finds it, and no one shall open the casket until we stand before the wizard himself.'

'But how will the dwarf know whether the stone is a ruby or not?' asked the queen. 'If he is blind he won't be able to tell.'

'Oh, don't make difficulties,' said the king, snappily.

'I'm doing my best.'

'But if the wizard opens the casket and sees a bit of coal there instead of a precious stone, he will be very angry,' said the queen. 'And how will you know what his thoughts are?'

'Oh, I'll think of those things on the journey,' said the king. 'It will take us six days, so there will be plenty of time to think.'

He sent the blind dwarf under the earth with a casket. Presently the little creature came back and gave the casket to the king. It rattled when he shook it and the king hoped that there was a beautiful ruby inside. He did not dare look, of course, for then somebody would have seen it.

He and the queen set off to Ho-Ho Land with all their court. There were a hundred and two travellers, some in coaches and some on horseback. They travelled slowly, for some of the roads were not good. On the way, the king tried to think of something he could ask the wizard to do which would be impossible. But he couldn't think of anything at all!

At last they all arrived in Ho-Ho Land. It was a strange country, with the sky very low so that it seemed more like a high ceiling than a sky. Far away on a mountain-top could be seen the wizard's magnificent castle, shining brightly, for it was made of gold mixed with blue glass.

The court halted at the foot of the mountain. It was drawing near night-time, too late to visit the wizard that day. The servants quickly put up the tents that the court had used for the last five nights, and prepared a meal. The king and queen dined with their nobles, and nobody dared say a word to the king, for he had been quite unable to think of how to fulfil the second and third conditions of the wizard, and was looking very worried indeed.

He was so worried that he could not sleep that night. When dawn came, he got up and slipped out of his tent. The sun was not yet risen, but the eastern sky was full of gold. He wandered up the hillside, gazing at the shining castle above him, trying in vain to think of something he could ask the wizard to do, which he would be unable to.

He sat down on a big stone, put his head into his hands and groaned loudly. He hadn't sat there for more than five minutes when he felt something licking his hand. He looked up and saw a fine sheepdog looking at him, with a very thick, curly coat. Just behind him was a bright-eyed shepherd lad with a crook.

'What ails you, master?' asked the shepherd, kindly. 'I and my dog, Curly, heard you groaning and sighing.'

'Ah, shepherd, you can do nothing to help me,' said the king. 'I and all my men whom you see down there will be servants of wizard Mighty-One before nightfall!'

'Well, why do you not run away?' asked the shepherd lad, in astonishment. 'There is plenty of time.'

'Alas! I cannot run away, because I have come to try to rescue my daughter, the Princess Mirabelle,' said the king. 'The wizard keeps her imprisoned in his castle. He will only let her go on three conditions – one, that I give him something no one else has ever seen – two, that I ask him to do a task he cannot do – three, that I tell him what his thoughts are when I am before him. The first condition I might manage, though it is hard enough, but the other two are too difficult for me.'

The shepherd laughed.

'They seem to me to be easy,' he said. 'I could do them all – of that I'm sure!'

The king stared at him in astonishment. 'Well, do them!' he said at last. 'Do them, shepherd, and maybe you shall have my beautiful daughter to be your wife!'

'Done!' said the shepherd. 'I have seen the lovely princess looking out of her tower window many a time this last month, and I would do anything in the world for her. But listen, O King – will you permit me to wear your tunic, cloak and crown, and pretend to be you today? For only if I do that can I outwit the wizard.'

'Anything you like!' cried the king. 'I will go and tell my courtiers now.'

Off he went, the shepherd following nimbly, the curly-haired sheepdog gambolling after. In a few words the king told his nobles what was going to happen. They agreed to follow the shepherd that day, and to pretend that he was the king himself.

'But, woe betide him if he does not do all he says!' said the oldest courtier, feeling his sword. 'For I will slay him if he has deceived you, O King!'

The king stripped off his silver tunic and took off his cloak of gold. He handed them to the shepherd who put them on. Then he took the king's glittering crown and placed that on his curly locks. A fine king he made, there was no mistake about that!

The king donned a suit belonging to one of his

courtiers, and mixed with them. Then up the hill the shepherd went, leading the way to the towering castle of glass and gold. He picked something from a bush on his way and put it into his pocket. The king could not see what it was. The shepherd hummed a jolly tune as he went, and the king felt lighter of heart than he had been for months!

At last they stood before the great wooden door of the castle. The big nails that studded the door were of shining gold. The shepherd knocked loudly.

The door swung open and the shepherd led the way in. The king and the courtiers looked round them in a scared manner as the great door swung to. They all wondered the same thing. Would they ever go out of that door – or would they have to stay inside as the wizard's servants for ever and ever?

The shepherd made his way into a room whose ceiling was so high that it seemed to be the sky. It was held up by tall, slender pillars, and from the top to the bottom of these pillars burnt green tongues of flame. At the end of the great room sat Wizard Mighty-One, giant-like in form, and with eyes that shone like pieces of glowing ember.

'So you have come!' he said to the shepherd, thinking he was the king. 'You think you can take your daughter from me by your cleverness? O King, you are very foolish. You and your nobles will be my servants, and the Princess Mirabelle will stay here all her life.'

'Not so!' said the shepherd, with a laugh. 'If I pit my wits against yours, O Mighty-One, I shall defeat you! Mirabelle shall leave this castle with me today!'

Mighty-One frowned and the flames that burnt all the way up the pillars turned from green to red.

'You have three conditions to fulfil,' he said sharply. 'What was the first?'

'The first, O wizard, was that I should bring to you something that no one else in the world has ever set eyes on before,' said the shepherd, bowing.

'Ho!' said the wizard, mockingly. 'And what have

you brought me? Some precious stone from under the earth? Some marvel from beneath the seas? None will be of use, for at some time or another worms or beetles see everything under the ground, and fishes swim around everything in the sea.'

'Nay, I bring you something that no man, bird, animal or insect has ever seen,' said the shepherd. He put his hand into his tunic pocket and brought out a brown hazel-nut!

'Open this shell, Mighty-One,' he said, 'and inside you will see a close-hidden nut, seen by no eyes but yours before.'

He placed the nut in the long-fingered hand of the suprised wizard. Mighty-One frowned again and the flames, climbing the pillars, changed from red to purple. It was enough to make anyone shake with fear.

But the shepherd did not care. He smiled impudently at the angry wizard, and offered to crack the nut for him.

'Enough!' said the wizard, angrily. 'I will not crack

the nut. There is no need. I will accept the first condition as fulfilled. You have brought me something that certainly no eyes have seen before – the kernel of this nut. Now what was the second condition?'

'The second condition, O Mighty-One, was that I should ask you to do something you could not do,' said the shepherd, his bright eyes twinkling.

'Ho!' said Mighty-One, pleased. 'That is impossible!'

The shepherd turned and whistled low. His sheepdog, Curly, ran up to him. The shepherd plucked a long, curling hair from his coat.

He gave it to the wizard.

'Straighten this hair for me,' he said.

The wizard looked at the shepherd as if he were mad. He took the hair and pulled it straight but it immediately shot back into a curl again. He flattened it under his hand – it went back curly again. He took an iron from the air by magic and slowly ironed the curly hair up and down – but the more he ironed it, the curlier it became!

Then in a rage he wetted his finger and damped that curly hair – but as soon as it dried it sprang back into a tighter curl than ever!

He called magic to his help and muttered strings of enchanted words. The hair gradually became straight – but as soon as the wizard stopped muttering the words the hair curled again so tightly that there was no straightening it at all!

The wizard threw down the hair in a rage and stamped his foot! The flames round the pillars shot up higher than ever and turned to orange, so that all the courtiers and the king trembled where they stood. Only the shepherd, grand in his cloak of gold and his bright crown, stood unafraid, smiling broadly.

'The second condition is fulfilled,' said the wizard at last, in a furious voice. 'You are cleverer than I thought you, O King. What was the third condition?'

'That I should tell you what you are thinking, O Mighty-One,' said the shepherd.

'That is impossible,' said the wizard, looking triumphantly at the shepherd. 'No one can tell me what I am thinking.'

The shepherd laughed loudly. His sides shook and his laugh echoed all round the great room. The king, hidden among his courtiers, wondered what there was to laugh at. He had watched the shepherd in wondering surprise when he fulfilled first one and then two of the wizard's conditions – but he did not see how the shepherd was going to defeat the wizard for the third time.

'Why do you laugh?' asked the wizard, angrily. 'You will not be so merry when you find yourself and all your men my servants, prisoners in my castle! Why do you laugh, I say?'

'I laugh because I know your thoughts!' said the shepherd. 'I know what you think, O Mighty-One! Your thoughts are easy to read!'

'What am I thinking then?' cried the wizard in a rage.

'O wizard, you are thinking that I am the king!' cried the shepherd. 'But I am not! I am only Strong-Arm, the shepherd!'

He pulled off his cloak and tunic and stood there in his rough jersey and thick hose, laughing at the astonished wizard.

'Tell truly!' he cried. 'You were thinking I was the king! Ah, I have read your thoughts, you see, Mighty-One! The third condition is fulfilled!'

The wizard saw that he was defeated. He gave a great howl and leapt up from his seat. There came a noise of thunder and the flames round the tall pillars roared like a fire. The castle shook and shivered and suddenly broke into a thousand pieces that flew away into the air, taking the wizard with them. Nothing was left at all, except the seat on which the wizard had sat.

The king, the shepherd and the courtiers were thrown to the ground. They leapt up at once and watched the castle and the wizard vanishing in the distance. Then the king remembered his daughter, the Princess Mirabelle.

'She has been spirited away, too!' he cried – but she hadn't. She suddenly appeared nearby and ran to the king in delight, hugging and kissing him.

'Oh, Father, I am free at last!' she cried. Then she curtsied to the shepherd and thanked him for all he had done for her, for, without him knowing it, she had heard everything from a nearby room.

Then, gladly and merrily, the king and queen, the shepherd, the Princess and the courtiers set off home again. How glad they were to see the last of the lowering skies of Ho-Ho Land! Their people welcomed them home in delight, for they had been certain that they would never again see either the king or his daughter.

Princess Mirabelle fell in love with the bright-eyed shepherd long before she reached home, and in a short time they were married. Every bell in the land rang out on their wedding-day, and so loud was the noise that the wizard Mighty-One, brooding in a faraway land, heard the joyful sound and frowned fiercely.

But he could do them no harm. He had been conquered by the sharp wits of a shepherd lad, and never again would he show his face to friend or foe.

Mr Hoo-Ha's
New Suit

Mr Hoo-Ha's New Suit

MR HOO-HA was a vain little gnome. He loved to have everything just a bit nicer than anyone else, so that he could boast about it. He liked to have the shiniest mackintosh, the biggest umbrella, the tallest top hat, and the most pointed shoes. He liked to have the biggest cucumbers in his garden, and the highest sunflowers. He was that kind of person.

Nobody liked him very much, and they used to laugh at him behind his back. But Mr Hoo-Ha didn't know that. He thought that everyone looked up to him and said he was the smartest gnome in Fiddle-Dee Village.

Ah! But just wait a minute, Mr Hoo-Ha. Pride comes before a fall, you know – so be careful!

Now one day the Smiling Witch thought she would give a party. Everyone loved her parties, for the Smiling Witch was a kind old dame, and liked people to have a good time. She often asked the Prince and Princess of Elfland, and the Lord of Feefo and the Lady of Fum, so the folk of Fiddle-Dee Village always put on their very best clothes when they went to the parties given by the Smiling Witch.

When Mr Hoo-Ha got his invitation card he was most excited. 'I shall have a wonderful new suit made!' he said to himself. 'Oh, a marvellous one! I shall be smarter than anyone else! I wonder what I can have it made of. I should like to find something quite new. I think I will go off in the bus to the world of boys and girls and see if I can pick up anything there.' So off he went in the bus.

When he got to our world, he found it covered

in white snow, for there had been a snowstorm the night before.

Mr Hoo-Ha stared at the snow in delight and amazement. He had never seen snow before. He put out his hand and felt it. It was very soft.

'Just the thing for my new suit!' said Mr Hoo-Ha to himself. 'Just the very thing! Pure white! No one will have pure white. And so soft! Like a duck's down. My, I shall be very smart and unusual this time!'

He took out his scissors and cut three and a half yards of snow. He rolled it up and packed it in a bag. Then he caught the next bus back to Fiddle-Dee Village and went straight to the tailor's.

The tailor was surprised to see such soft, white stuff. 'It will be difficult to make up into a suit, Mr Hoo-Ha,' he said.

'That's your business,' said Hoo-Ha. 'I pay you for doing that, don't I? Well, just get on with your work, then, and make me a fine suit – the finest you have ever made.'

The tailor did his best. It was really very difficult, for the needle slid in and out of the snow, and until the tailor used a special frosty thread he could not seem to sew the snow together. But at last the suit was made, and delivered to Mr Hoo-Ha's house.

'Good!' said Hoo-Ha, turning the soft, shining suit out of the box. 'Very good! It looks lovely!'

When the night of the party came Mr Hoo-Ha had a bath, and then put on his vest. It was rather dirty and had some holes in it – for although Hoo-Ha was most particular about his suits and hats, he didn't mind very much about the things he wore underneath.

'After all, nobody ever sees those!' he said. 'I can't be bothered to keep washing and mending my vests. So long as I am nice on top, it doesn't matter what I'm like underneath!'

So, even for the party, he put on his dirty and holey old vest. And then he put on his new snow-suit! My, you should have seen it! It was so soft, so white – and how it glittered! It was the loveliest suit ever seen in Fiddle-Dee Village.

Mr Hoo-Ha put on his new white hat to match and went off to the party. How he twirled his stick as he went along! How he stuck out his toes!

But the new suit was rather cold. It made Mr Hoo-Ha shiver. His nose turned blue with cold. His fingers could hardly take hold of his stick.

'It's a c-c-c-cold n-n-n-night!' said Mr Hoo-Ha, his teeth chattering.

The Smiling Witch greeted him kindly. Everyone else had arrived, for Hoo-Ha always liked to come in last, because then, you see, everybody could see how grand he looked! The Smiling Witch took him by the hand and led him to the fire.

'You are cold, Mr Hoo-Ha!' she said. 'Dear me, you are shivering! Come and warm yourself! What a wonderful new suit you are wearing! I have never seen anything like it before!'

'It certainly is beautiful,' said everyone, in wonder.

Mr Hoo-Ha felt very grand. He turned himself all round so that everyone could see him.

'Yes,' he said. 'It's the very latest fashion. You ought to have some dresses made of it, Smiling Witch. It costs a lot of money, this stuff, but still, it's worth it.'

Now this was a naughty story, for Mr Hoo-Ha had simply cut the snow off the ground for his new suit. But nobody knew that, so he just went on boasting for all he was worth. He still felt very cold, and he stood in front of the Smiling Witch's big fire, warming himself all over.

And then a strange and curious thing began to happen. Hoo-Ha's lovely new suit began to disappear! It turned into water and dripped off him! You see, it was made of snow – and so, of course, the hot fire melted it! Mr Hoo-Ha looked down in surprise when he felt something dripping down his legs!

'Your suit's melting! Your suit's melting!' cried all the little folk. 'Oh, look!'

There was no stopping it. It went on melting till it was all gone – and there stood poor Mr Hoo-Ha in front of the fire, with nothing on but a dirty and very holey vest!

'Why don't you mend your vest?' cried the little folk, in disgust. 'What's the use of wearing grand things on top, if you're shabby underneath! For shame, Mr Hoo-Ha! Look at your holey vest! You're nothing but a boaster, Mr Hoo-Ha! Go home and mend your vest!'

Well, that was the end of Hoo-Ha's boasting. It was a long time before he went to a party again – but when he did, he went early, and sat in a corner, and he wore clothes just about the same as other people, no finer and no smarter. And underneath he was neat and clean, so you see he had learnt his lesson! Poor Mr Hoo-Ha!

It's Going
to Rain!

It's Going to Rain!

OLD DAME Twinkle didn't know *what* to do with her dreamy husband. He did do such silly things. He never thought about what he was doing, and so he used to brush his hair with his toothbrush, clean his boots with the grate-polish and look for hens' eggs in the dog-kennel. So you can guess what a bother he was to look after.

The thing that worried Dame Twinkle most of all was the habit Mr Twinkle had of going out for a walk, carrying his umbrella and mackintosh – and then, if it rained, he came back *still* carrying his umbrella and mackintosh! And, of course, he was wet through!

'Twinkle, why *don't* you put on your mackintosh and put up your umbrella when it rains?' Dame Twinkle would cry in despair. 'What is the sense of taking them if you don't use them? Can't you *see* when it is going to rain and *feel* when it is pouring down?'

'I don't walk with my eyes on the sky all the time,' said Mr Twinkle. 'A-*tish*-oo!'

'There! You've got *another* cold,' said Dame Twinkle. 'Off to bed with you!'

Well, you can imagine that Dame Twinkle was very worried about her husband always catching colds because he got wet through so often. And at last she went to Witch Green-Eyes to ask her for a spell to stop Mr Twinkle from being so foolish.

'I can't give you a spell for that,' said Witch Green-Eyes. 'It is the hardest thing in the world to stop a stupid person from being foolish. It can't be done.'

'Well, what can I do, then?' said poor Dame Twinkle. 'There he goes, out for his walk, his eyes on the ground all the time! He never thinks of looking up to see what the weather is like!'

'If he looks at the ground all the time, why not put something there to warn him!' said the witch. 'Leave it to me, Dame Twinkle. I will think of something.'

So she thought hard; and then she went down the lanes and through the fields where Mr Twinkle loved to walk, carrying a pot of bright scarlet paint. With it she painted the petals of a small white flower that grew by the wayside, and into the flower she put a rain-spell so that it would close up its petals tightly whenever rain was near.

Then she called on Dame Twinkle. 'Tell your husband to watch the bright scarlet flower by the wayside,' she said. 'Red for danger, you know! When it closes its petals, rain is coming – so Mr Twinkle will be warned and will put on his mackintosh in time!'

And now Mr Twinkle has no more colds, because the little flower always warns him when rain is near. Do you know what its name is? It is the scarlet pimpernel, and it still has some of the old magic in it – for, as you will see, it closes its red petals tightly whenever rain is near!

The Enchanted
Forest

The Enchanted Forest

ROLAND AND Gilly often used to stay with their Uncle Dru and their Auntie Rosalind. They loved going there because their uncle and aunt lived in a cottage on the edge of a big forest, and Uncle Dru could tell all sorts of strange, exciting stories of what went on there.

'There's odd folk in that forest,' he would say. 'My, there are brownies, goblins, gnomes and I don't know what besides, to say nothing of an odd witch or two. It's at the end of the world we live, and all sorts of forgotten folk peep out of that forest at times.'

'Oooh! I wish we could see them!' said Roland, but

Uncle Dru shook his big head.

'Now don't you go seeking anything in the forest,' he said. 'There's plenty of adventures to be found there I've no doubt, but they're not the sort for you!'

'Gilly, come and help me with the baking,' called Auntie Rosalind.

'And you, Roland, come and help me with my digging,' said Uncle Dru.

'Oh, it's such a nice day, couldn't Gilly and I go off for the day and have a holiday?' asked Roland, looking longingly at the sunny lane outside the garden.

'Perhaps tomorrow,' said Uncle Dru. 'Today there is a lot to be done.'

That was the worst of Uncle Dru and Auntie Rosalind. They always found so many jobs for the two children. There seemed to be such a lot to do, and Gilly and Roland hardly ever had time to go off by themselves. Still, never mind, perhaps they could tomorrow. Gilly ran indoors to help with the baking, and Roland found a spade to help with the digging.

'You know,' said Uncle Dru, as they set to work, 'I used to have a most wonderful spade, Roland. My, it was a marvel, that spade was!'

'What could it do?' asked Roland, in surprise.

'Why, I had only to say, "Dig, spade, dig, for your life!" and it would set to work and dig all my garden by itself!' said Uncle Dru. 'It saved me such a lot of work!'

'What happened to it?' asked Roland, in excitement. 'Oh, I do wish I could see it!'

'Oh, a witch came by one night when I had left it out, and she took it,' said Uncle Dru, sadly. 'I've never seen it since!'

'I *must* tell Gilly that story,' said Roland. 'I'm sure she's never heard such a strange tale in her life!'

But Gilly had! She was listening to one that very minute. She had been helping her aunt to mix the butter and flour for the cakes, and had been stirring the dinner cooking in the pot.

'Once,' said Auntie Rosalind, suddenly, 'once, dear

child, I had a most wonderful pot. Oh, it was a marvel, that pot! You could put anything you liked into it – maybe just one potato, a bit of onion and a bone – and it would turn it into the finest meal you could think of! Fit for a king, with a smell that would make you so hungry you couldn't wait another minute for your dinner!'

'Oooh!' said Gilly, in surprise. 'I wish I could have seen it! Did it wear out?'

'No,' said her aunt. 'Pots like that never wear out. No, my dear, I washed it one evening and put it out on the sill to dry. A witch came by that same night and stole it. I've never seen it since.'

'I really must tell Roland that strange story,' said Gilly, excitedly. 'Fancy! A real magic pot that could cook a dinner out of almost nothing!'

When the children had each finished their work they ran to tell one another what they had heard about the magic spade and pot. How surprised they were to hear each other's story!

'I wish we could find the witch that stole those things,' said Roland. 'I'd love to take them away from her! Gilly! Shall we go into the forest tomorrow, and see if we can find where she lives?'

'I'd be frightened to,' said Gilly, going red with excitement. 'But oh, I'd love to!'

When the next day came, it was pouring with rain. What a disappointment!

'You certainly can't go out today,' said Auntie Rosalind. 'It's too wet. You must stay in.'

'It's a good chance for you to learn basket-making,' said Uncle Dru to Roland. 'I'll teach you.'

'And it's a good chance for you to learn knitting!' said Auntie Rosalind to Gilly. 'I'll teach you!'

'Oh, Auntie, oh Uncle, we don't want to learn anything today!' cried the children. 'Can't we read?'

'No,' said Uncle Dru, firmly. 'Basket-making might be very useful to you one day. You simply never know!'

'And knitting may be very *very* useful to you some

day,' said Auntie Rosalind. 'You simply never know!'

That's what Uncle Dru and Auntie Rosalind always said when they wanted to teach something to Gilly and Roland. 'You simply never know when it will come in useful!'

'I'm sure I shall never want to make baskets,' said Roland.

'You don't know!' said Uncle Dru, taking some cane out of the water in which it had been soaking. 'I shouldn't be surprised if one day you aren't very glad indeed you learnt to make baskets.'

Uncle Dru's words came true, though Roland didn't think they would, as he sat rather sulkily learning how to weave the cane this way and that until he had made a fine little basket. Gilly sat patiently learning how to knit, and when the next day and the day after that both turned out to be wet, the children got on very well indeed with their new tasks.

Then there came a beautiful sunny day.

'You've been good, patient children, so you may go

out this morning,' said Auntie Rosalind. 'Be back for dinner. Here is an apple for you, Gilly, and one for you, Roland. Now be sure not to go into the forest!'

Off went the children – and oh dear, they disobeyed! Yes, they went into the forest by the very first path they saw! Wasn't it naughty of them?

They felt tremendously excited. They meant to find the witch who had stolen their uncle's spade, and their auntie's cooking pot. They felt certain that it was the same witch who had stolen both things.

Presently they came to a curious house. It was built of round cobblestones. There were some of red, some of yellow and some of blue. The chimney pot was black and looked for all the world like a big top hat set on the roof. Gilly felt quite sure it *was*.

'Let's knock at the door and ask if anyone round about here has a magic spade and cooking pot,' said Gilly. So they went up the little front path and knocked on the door.

A goblin woman came to the door. She had long,

pointed ears, bright green eyes and a cross mouth. Round her head was a green scarf, and in her hand was a broom.

'What do you want?' she asked, crossly. 'I'm in the middle of my dusting. This is a silly time to call!'

'I'm sorry,' said Roland. 'But I just wanted to ask if you knew of anyone in the forest who has a magic spade that will dig by itself and a magic cooking pot that will cook a dinner out of nothing.'

'That's easy,' said the goblin woman. 'Why, everyone knows that Dame Tantrums has them! Where do you come from that you don't know that? If you want to borrow them, it's no good asking her, because she won't lend them. I've often tried to get them for a day myself, but the mean old thing won't let them out of her sight!'

Roland and Gilly felt excited at this news. So there really was a witch who had their uncle's spade and their auntie's cooking pot!

'Could you tell me where Dame Tantrums lives?'

asked Roland, politely.

'Follow the blue buttercups, and they will take you to her tower,' said the goblin woman. 'I should have thought you would have known that. Now, I can't stand here talking any longer, I've my dusting to do and seven children coming home from school in an hour. Good day to you!'

She slammed the door and the two children ran down the path. They had found out all they wanted to know!

'Where are the blue buttercups?' wondered Gilly, looking all round. 'Oh, look! There's one!'

She pointed to a strange buttercup not far off. It was bright blue. Another one was a little further on, and a third one further on still.

'This is the way!' said Gilly, dancing to the buttercups. Sure enough, it was! There were dozens and dozens of blue buttercups growing in a line through the trees and the children followed them for quite a mile.

Suddenly they came to a curious tower. It was built of pale blue stones, and had one little window right at the very top. There was a strange round door at the bottom, which was wide open.

'This must be where Dame Tantrums lives,' said Gilly. 'Let's knock!'

But nobody came in answer to their knock. 'Let's go in and see if we can find Uncle's spade and Auntie's cooking pot!' said Roland. So they crept inside the tower, and looked around. But all they could see was a stone stairway winding round and round inside the tower. They went up it and up and up, and at the very top they found a door. It was open and they looked inside.

They saw a square room, with a bright fire burning at one side. There was a round table there, and a chair and two stools. A big bed stood in one corner, and a dresser with blue and yellow plates was in another.

Over the fire hung a black cooking pot, and Gilly was quite sure it was her aunt's! And in the corner by the dresser stood a big spade!

'That's Uncle's spade!' cried Roland, and ran to get it. But oh my goodness me! At that very moment, who should come in at the door but Dame Tantrums herself, the old witch! She stood and glared at the two children, then, quick as lightning, she slammed the door and locked it!

'Ho!' she said. 'So you thought you'd come and get my spade and my cooking pot, did you? Well, you've come, and now you'll stay!'

'No, please let us go,' begged Roland, feeling frightened. 'We wouldn't like to stay in this tower.'

'It doesn't matter whether you like it or not,' said the witch. 'I shall keep you here until I go to the Never-Never Land, and then I'll take you with me and sell you to the Never-Nevers!'

So the two children were kept prisoners in the tall tower. They were very miserable, especially as there were no books to read and no toys to play with. Gilly had to keep the room tidy, and Roland had to look after the fire, but that didn't take very long.

'I can't have you wasting your time like this,' said the witch. 'Can't you do something? Can you sew, girl?'

'Not very well,' said Gilly.

'Well, can you knit, then?'

'Yes, I can knit,' said Gilly. So the witch got out great balls of coloured wools and a pair of enormous golden needles. She gave them to Gilly and told her to knit a winter scarf.

'What can *you* do?' she asked Roland.

'I can dig,' said Roland.

'Ho!' said Dame Tantrums, 'well you won't dig in *my* garden! You'd escape, I know, if I let you down the stairs! Can you make baskets?'

'Yes,' said Roland, remembering his uncle's lessons. The witch pulled out some cane from a cupboard and put it into a bowl of water to soak.

'You can make me a washing-basket,' she said. 'Now, listen – I am going away for three days, and when I come back I want to find that scarf done and that basket finished.'

She put on her tall witch's hat, wound her cloak round her and unlocked the door. She locked it again on the other side, and the children heard her going down the steps. They leant out of the window and saw her flying away on a crooked broomstick.

They each started their work – and suddenly Gilly had an idea!

'I say, Roland! I believe that in three days, if I work very hard, I could make a scarf long enough to use as a rope to let down from the window to the ground!' said Gilly, excitedly.

'Ooh! What a good idea! And oh Gilly! I could make a basket to let down the cooking pot and the spade in!' said Roland. So they both set to work again with a will, and how excited they felt! If only they could get the knitted rope done before the witch came back, and if only they could let down the stolen things in Roland's basket, and take them back to their aunt and uncle!

All day long and far into the night the two children worked. At last they fell asleep over their work, and didn't wake up until the sun streamed in through the little window. Then they set to work again. Roland's basket was finished first, and he put into it the cooking pot and spade. But the basket wasn't quite big enough so he added to it.

Gilly let down the knitted scarf from the window, and found that she had knitted just over half the length she needed. So she set to work again and knitted at top speed.

'Aunt and Uncle were right,' she said to Roland. 'You simply never know when anything is going to come in useful! What a good thing I learnt knitting the other day, and you learnt to make baskets!'

When the third day came, the scarf reached nearly to the ground and Gilly knitted faster than ever to finish it before the witch came back that night. At last, just as the sun was setting, it was the right length!

'We shall have to be quick,' said Roland. 'The witch

may be back at any minute now!'

They tied the top of the scarf to a big nail just inside the window, and then dropped the rest of it outside. It just reached the ground!

'You go down first,' said Roland to Gilly. 'Then I'll let down the basket with the cooking pot and spade inside, and come down myself.'

So Gilly climbed outside the window, and swung herself on to the knitted scarf. Down she went, hand over hand, and at last reached the ground. Then Roland pulled up the scarf and tied his basket on to the end of it. He let it down and Gilly untied it when it reached her. Then Roland climbed down the scarf himself, and there they were, side by side on the ground below!

'Good!' said Roland. 'Now quick! We must get away as fast as we can in case the witch comes back!'

They ran off quickly, Gilly carrying the cooking pot and Roland carrying the spade. They followed the blue buttercups till they came to the house of the goblin woman. Then they knew their way home quite well.

Just as they got to the edge of the forest, who should they see flying in the air but Dame Tantrums herself! She saw them and gave a howl of rage. The children ran out of the forest towards their uncle's cottage as fast as they could. The witch knew that she could not catch them, and sailed off to her tower muttering angrily.

'Uncle Dru! Auntie Rosalind! We've come back home and brought your magic cooking pot and magic spade!' cried Roland.

How worried their aunt and uncle had been, and how glad they were to see Roland and Gilly! They hugged and kissed them, and said they were wonderful children, and quite forgave them for being disobedient and going into the forest.

Roland and Gilly told them all their adventures, and when their uncle and aunt heard about the knitting and the basket-making, how astonished they were.

'Well, there!' they cried. 'What did we tell you? Didn't we say, "You simply never know when anything will come in useful!" What would you have done if you couldn't knit or make a basket?'

They were so glad to get back their magic spade and cooking pot. Uncle Dru went digging in his garden that very same evening with it, and Auntie Rosalind threw an old potato, a cabbage leaf and a mutton bone into the pot – and hey presto! it made the most delicious stew they had ever tasted!

'Well, well,' said Uncle Dru, when they all sat down to it. 'You simply NEVER know!'

The Sulkabit
Wizard

The Sulkabit Wizard

ONCE UPON a time there lived a wizard called Sulkabit. He really ought to have been called Sulka*lot*, because he was forever frowning and growling and sulking.

He lived in the village of Merryheart. It wasn't a very big village, but everybody was merry there, for it was the prettiest, sunniest little spot in the whole of Fairyland.

The happiest person there was plump Mother Runaround. She lived all alone in Laughing Cottage at the end of the village. Everybody liked her because she was always running around doing all sorts of odd jobs for this person and that, and she always had a large smile ready for anybody she met.

No, I shouldn't have said *every*body liked her because one person didn't, and that was the Sulkabit Wizard. He couldn't bear her because she laughed at him.

He was always shaking his head and saying something terrible was going to happen, and Mother Runaround would never believe him.

'I'm sure there will be an earthquake tomorrow,' he said. 'If not here, then somewhere else. It would be more fitting for you to sigh than to laugh, Mother Runaround.'

'Bless my button boots!' cried Mother Runaround, setting her basket down. 'What happened to the great black storm you said was going to come last week? And what about the plague of caterpillars you told me of? *I* never saw anything of them.'

'They happened somewhere,' said the Sulkabit Wizard, crossly, 'and they might have happened here, for all *you* were to know!'

'I'll wait till they come, then, before I begin to worry!' laughed Mother Runaround. 'You're a funny sort of person to live in the Village of Merryheart, Sulkabit! You ought to go and live in Doleful Town, where everyone sighs and groans, instead of laughs!'

And with that, Mother Runaround picked up her basket and went off to give a pot of her new honey to Hoppetty Ho, who lived at the top of the hill.

Sulkabit looked after her. He saw a tribe of little pixies dance up to her and take her basket from her to carry. He saw Fairy Tiptoes fly up and kiss her. He saw Toddles, the baby of the village, run up and give her a bunch of flowers out of his very own garden.

'*I* don't know why they all like her so much,' he grumbled. 'Nobody ever carries *my* basket for me, or gives *me* anything!'

Pinkity Pixie came trotting by him just then, and

the Sulkabit Wizard called out to him.

'Hey, Pinkity! Come and carry my basket for me. Why don't you help me as you help Mother Runaround?'

'Ho, help the Sulkabit Wizard!' laughed Pinkity. 'Not I! Your frowns and groans are enough to chase anyone away, and we all know that some of your magic is bad magic! *We* don't want to be turned into beetles and toads!'

He ran away, laughing, and Sulkabit was left standing alone, looking as cross as two sticks.

It was quite true that some of his magic was bad magic. When he had been cross with the Knobbly Gnome, he had put a bad spell in the gnome's front garden, and all his cabbages grew prickles, so that the Knobbly Gnome couldn't pick them, and was as frightened as could be.

And another time he had done a bad turn to the Bee-Woman, and made all her honey turn pink, so that she was afraid to eat it.

The Sulkabit Wizard went home, muttering and grumbling, wishing he could do Mother Runaround a bad turn too.

'I must be careful, though,' he said to himself, 'for if anyone guesses I have done it, I shall be turned out of Merryheart Village, there's no doubt of that.'

So he sat down and he thought and thought what he could do, and at last he thought of a plan.

'Ho, ho!' he chuckled. 'Ho, ho! I'll make a cake and I'll put a spell in it. Then I'll take the cake to Mother Runaround and give it to her. When she eats it the spell will work, and no one will know anything about how she got it!'

What do you think the spell was? It was that anyone who ate the cake should at once begin to give away every single thing in the house, and only stop when there was nothing left at all!

'Ho, ho!' chuckled the wizard again. 'I'd like to see old Mother Runaround's face when she sees herself giving away her chairs and her tables, her pictures and her kettles! She *will* feel funny when she stands in the middle of her empty cottage. What fun it will be!'

He at once set to work to make the cake. It was quite an ordinary cake to look at, yellow inside and brown on top. Sulkabit baked it well, popped the spell inside, let it cool, and then wrapped it up in a newspaper.

'Perhaps I'd better not let Mother Runaround know it's from me,' he decided. 'She might think it rather funny.'

So he wrote a message on a card, and slipped it in the parcel. It just said 'From a friend' and nothing more.

That night, when it was dark, and everyone in Merryheart was asleep, the Sulkabit Wizard crept out of his cottage and went to Mother Runaround's. He put the parcel on her doorstep and then crept back to his cottage again.

'Now we shall see something funny soon!' he said, rubbing his hands together. 'Old Mother Runaround won't be laughing very much for a few weeks, and she will be very sorry she ever laughed at me!'

Now next morning, when Mother Runaround opened her door, she found the parcel.

'Dear me, whatever can this be?' she said, and took it indoors. She unpacked it, and found the cake with the message that said 'From a friend'.

'From a friend!' she said. 'Now whoever can that be, I wonder!'

She couldn't think who it could be, and she popped the cake into the larder for tea-time. But it hadn't been there very long when Mother Runaround remembered she had bought a fine new cake the day before.

'It does seem greedy to have two cakes in the house!' she said. 'I really think I must give one away to somebody. I'd better give the one I found on the doorstep, because I've cut a piece out of the other one.'

So she took it out of the larder, and set it on the table. She fetched a nice piece of white paper and wrapped it round the cake. Then she tied it with a bright piece of blue ribbon, for Mother Runaround didn't believe in wrapping a cake up in newspaper and dirty old string.

Then she set off to go to the Knobbly Gnome's at the other end of the village. When she got there she found he was out, so she left the cake on his kitchen table with a note to say that it was for him.

'I don't expect he gets many cakes,' she said to herself as she went home, 'so I think he'll be very pleased.'

When the Knobbly Gnome got home, he undid the parcel and found the cake.

'Dear, dear!' he said. 'A fine new cake from Mother Runaround, and I'm going away tomorrow so I can't eat it! What a pity! Never mind, I'll give it to someone else. I know she won't mind.'

He wrapped it up again, and wondered whom to take it to.

'I'll give it to the Fiddle-de-dee Elf!' he decided.

'She is not very well, so she will be pleased to have a nice present.'

He popped it into a basket and ran off. The Fiddle-de-dee Elf's servant came to the door when he got there and took the parcel from the Knobbly Gnome.

She ran to give it to the elf, who was in bed, feeling rather weak.

'A present!' cried the little servant.

The Fiddle-de-dee Elf untied the blue ribbon and unwrapped the cake.

'Oh!' she cried. 'It's a lovely cake – but oh dear me, the doctor says I'm not to eat cake for a whole week! How very, very disappointing!'

'Give it to Greeneyes the Goblin,' said the little servant. 'It's his birthday today!'

'Wrap it up again and take it to him, then,' said the elf. 'He will love it.'

The servant wrapped it up again neatly, put on her hat, and ran off. Greeneyes lived quite near, so it wasn't very long before she had knocked at the door and delivered the parcel.

Greeneyes wondered what it could be. He opened it, and groaned when he saw the cake.

'That's the fifth cake I've had given me for my birthday!' he said. 'Whatever shall I do with it? I really can't eat five. I must give it away to someone else.'

He tied it up again and wondered whom to take it to.

'I'll give it to Frisky the Squirrel,' he decided. 'He's a dear little fellow, and I'm sure he'll like it.'

So off he went with the cake.

But Frisky had gone to sleep for the winter and didn't want to wake up again yet.

'Cake!' he said sleepily. 'Don't want cake now, Greeneyes. Give it to the Skippitty Pixie, who lives in the next tree to mine.'

Greeneyes went to the next tree, and found Skippitty was not there.

He saw a note stuck up on the tree. It said:

THE SULKABIT WIZARD

GONE OUT

BACK SOON.

'Oh well, I'll pop the cake inside his door,' thought Greeneyes, 'and he'll find it when he comes back.'

So he put the cake down and went home again.

Very soon Skippitty came home, and nearly fell over the cake inside his door.

'What in the world is this?' he cried, and picked it up. He put it on his little table and unwrapped it.

'A cake!' he cried. 'And oh dear, I hate cake! What a pity it wasn't biscuits! Whatever shall I do with it?'

He sat down and thought.

'I'll go and give it to the Sulkabit Wizard!' he said at last. 'Nobody ever has a kind word for him, and maybe this will make him glad.'

So he carefully wrapped the cake up again in its nice white paper, and tied the blue ribbon round it. Then he put on his little pointed cap and set off for the Wizard's cottage.

When he got there he knocked loudly. The wizard came to the door.

'I've brought a present for you,' said Skippitty, rather nervously. 'I hope you will like it.'

The Sulkabit Wizard took the parcel, muttered a grumpy thank you, and shut the door.

He put the parcel down on the table. He was really rather excited about it, for he hadn't had a present for a very long time.

'I hope it's something to eat,' he said, 'because I really feel rather hungry, and there's only dry bread in the cupboard!'

He opened the parcel and found the cake. He didn't guess for one moment that it was the very same cake he had made the day before. He thought that that cake was safely at Mother Runaround's, waiting to be eaten.

'A cake!' he cried. 'Just what I wanted! I'll make a good meal of it.'

He fetched a knife, cut the cake, and ate a

large slice. It was good, so he ate another. Then he ate a third.

'I may as well eat the lot,' he said. 'It's not a very big cake.'

So he ate it all. Little did he know that a powerful spell was mixed in with it!

Soon the spell began to work. The wizard looked around his room.

'I think I'll take that nice cosy little chair of mine and give it to Mother Runaround,' he found himself saying.

Then, to his own great surprise, his legs walked over to the chair, his hands picked it up, and off he went to Laughing Cottage. He didn't really want to go one bit, but he couldn't help it.

When he got there his tongue said, 'This is for you, Mother Runaround, with my love,' and his hands pushed the chair into Mother Runaround's cottage.

Mother Runaround was tremendously astonished. She took the chair, and stared at Sulkabit.

'Perhaps he's sorry he's so sulky and cross,' she thought to herself. 'Perhaps he's trying to make up for it. I must be nice to him.'

So she smiled kindly at him, and thanked him in her nicest voice.

Sulkabit went back to his cottage, and took up a table. He went with it to Hoppetty Ho's, all the way up the hill, and gave it to him. He didn't want to, but he really couldn't help it. He was most astonished at himself, and he couldn't think what had happened to him.

He gave away all his chairs, his bed, his carpet, his pictures, his kettles and his crockery. He gave his books to Greeneyes and his clock to Fiddle-de-dee.

Everybody was surprised at him, for all in Merryheart Village knew him to be a cross and surly old wizard. Still, everyone thought he was trying his best to be kind and generous, and they smiled at him and thanked him very prettily. Some of them kissed him, and Sulkabit was surprised to find he liked it.

'It's really very nice to be smiled at and kissed,' he thought. 'No wonder Mother Runaround always laughs and looks happy, for everyone smiles at her and loves her. But whatever can be the matter with me? I seem to be under a magic spell.'

Not until Sulkabit's cottage was quite empty, and he stood lonely and puzzled in the middle of his bare floor, did he guess what had happened to him.

'I've eaten my own cake!' he suddenly groaned. 'Yes, that's what I've done! That cake must have been the one I made, but someone had wrapped it up in white paper and tied it with blue ribbon and I didn't think it was the same one. Oh dear, oh dear, I am punished indeed for my bad thoughts. Still, I have had more smiles and kisses today than Mother Runaround, I'm sure, and my heart is warm tonight, even if my hands are not.'

He shivered. Then he went out to the barn and took a great armful of hay. He made himself a bed on the bare floor, and went to sleep.

When Pop-in the postman called next morning, he was astonished to see Sulkabit lying asleep on the floor, with all his furniture gone. He called everyone to see, and soon all the village knew that Sulkabit had given away everything he had, and had nothing left for himself.

'We made a mistake about him,' they said in surprise. 'He is good and generous after all. Let's wake him and tell him we want to be friends with him.'

So for the first time in his life Sulkabit was awakened by kisses and kind names, and he could hardly believe his eyes and ears when he sat up and saw smiling, kindly faces all around him.

'We want to be friends with you, dear old Sulkabit,' said the little people.

Sulkabit remembered how he had been caught by his own spell – but he made up his mind never to tell anyone about it.

'I will be kind because I want to, now, not because of a spell,' he said to himself, and he smiled at everyone around him.

And from that very day he changed, and nobody ever knew why. Only *I* knew, and now I have told all the secret to you!

Gee Up, Old Clothes Horse!

Gee Up, Old Clothes Horse!

ONCE UPON a time the two pixies, Diddle and Pompetty, went to buy themselves new suits to go to Dame Twiddle's party. They went to Mr Snip the tailor, and he fitted them out with a marvellous suit each.

Diddle had a red suit with green buttons, and Pompetty had a green suit with red buttons. They each had a black hat with a feather in it, so you can guess they looked very smart!

When they walked out of the shop they looked at one another and laughed.

'You look like the King of Diddle,' said Pompetty.

'And you look as if you ought to be Lord High and Mighty Pompetty,' said Diddle. 'Let's pretend we are.'

So they took a walk through the woods, and sang as they went. This is what Diddle sang:

'I'm the King of Diddle,
Hie-tiddle-iddle-iddle!
I've a palace tall and fair
And a golden crown to wear,
Oh, I'm the King of Diddle,
Hie-diddle-iddle-iddle!'

Then Pompetty sang a little song he had made up. It went like this:

'Here comes Lord Pompetty,
Rich as can be,
Hey-derry, ho-derry,
Smick-a-smack-smee!

Look at me well,
I'm as grand as ten kings,
I've castles and cabbages,
Riches and rings!

Oh, here comes Lord Pompetty,
Rich as can be,
Hey-derry, ho-derry,
Smick-a-smack-smee!'

'That's a good song of yours,' said Diddle, 'especially the bit about smick-a-smack-smee. But cabbages don't seem to go with castles somehow.'

'No, they don't,' said Pompetty. 'But it was the only word I could think of just then.'

They went on through the wood, singing their songs, and everyone they met stopped and stared. Little elves bowed to them. Brownies cheered them. Diddle and Pompetty really did feel very grand indeed.

But suddenly they met the old enchanter, Little-Eyes. He was always on the look-out for riches, and when he heard the song of the two pixies his little eyes gleamed.

'Stars and moon, if only I could catch these two rich fellows, and hold them prisoner, I could get a lot of money out of them,' thought the enchanter to himself.

So he went up to them and bowed. 'Sirs,' he said, 'I have a fine carriage here for sale. Such great men as yourselves might like to buy it.'

'Well, no, thank you, we don't want a carriage today,' said Diddle.

'We've plenty at home,' said Pompetty, grandly and most untruthfully – but he was still pretending to be Lord Pompetty.

'Well, great sirs, will you not let me take you for a short ride?' said the artful enchanter. 'Perhaps you may have a friend who would like to buy it.'

Diddle and Pompetty had never ridden in a grand carriage in their lives. They simply longed to go in the enchanter's carriage. They could see it not far off between the trees – and it had four white owls for horses! Lovely!

'Well,' said Diddle, 'I don't mind if I do take a ride.'

So the two pixies got into the blue carriage, the enchanter whipped up the owls, and off they went in the air, over the tops of the trees. It was very pleasant.

'I think we'd better go back now,' said Diddle, after a while. 'We're going to a party this afternoon and it wouldn't do to be late.'

Little-Eyes the enchanter said nothing. He just whipped up his owls a bit faster. The two pixies suddenly felt scared. What was this old fellow up to? Surely he wasn't taking them away to keep? What good would that do him? Ah – but he thought they were a king and a lord! Of course! He meant to get money out of them.

Just then the owl-carriage dropped down to a big cottage standing on a hill by itself. The door opened; the owls flew in and took the carriage with them. It just got inside the door nicely. The door slammed shut behind it and the enchanter gave a laugh.

'Welcome!' he said to the pixies. 'I've caught you nicely, Your Majesty Diddle, and Your Highness Pompetty. Now you won't be able to get away unless you promise to give me a castle to live in, and ten sacks of gold to spend.'

The pixies stared at him in horror. 'Don't be silly,' said Diddle at last. 'We're only ordinary pixies. We're not really grand people. We were only pretending. After we've paid for these suits, which were new today, we shan't have a penny.'

'I don't believe that,' said Little-Eyes. 'I saw all the elves bowing to you, and heard the brownies cheering you in the wood. No – you won't trick me by pretending you are just ordinary pixies. I know you are rich and grand men.'

Well, nothing that Diddle or Pompetty could say would make Little-Eyes believe they were ordinary pixies. It was so tiresome, because the pixies knew that they would not be able to go to the party if Little-Eyes wouldn't let them go.

'I'll leave you to think things over by yourselves,' said the enchanter at last. 'You can go into the kitchen. It's nice and warm there – and you needn't try to get out of the window because there's a spell on it so that it can't be opened. I shall lock the door.'

So the two pixies found themselves prisoners in a warm kitchen. There certainly was a spell on the window, for it wouldn't move at all. Diddle and Pompetty stared at one another in dismay.

'We've been rather foolish,' said Diddle in a small voice. 'We shouldn't have been so vain. It looks as if we shall miss the party, Pompetty – so our new suits will be wasted.'

'Even if we could get out of the window, we've got no way of getting home,' said Pompetty gloomily. 'We've no horse – no bird – no aeroplane.'

They stared at the fire. A clothes horse stood in front with some handkerchiefs and collars on it, drying. An idea came to Diddle and he gave a squeal.

'Pompetty! Do you know enough magic to make this clothes horse come alive for a little while?'

'Yes!' shouted Pompetty, who was quite good at spells. He took a box from his pocket and dipped his finger into some ointment it held. He rubbed it carefully over the clothes horse. Then the two pixies danced solemnly round it and sang a song of strange magic words – and as they sang and danced, peculiar things happened to the clothes horse.

It grew a horse's head! It grew a long tail! Its legs grew longer and it began to paw the ground! It was a real clothes horse now, that could whinny and shake its mane and tail! The pixies jumped on its back and shouted in joy.

Just at that moment the enchanter opened the door to see what the noise was about – and that was the pixies' chance.

'Gee up, old clothes horse!' yelled Diddle, and the clothes horse geed up. It galloped at top speed to the door, knocked over Little-Eyes, and tore out of the cottage on its wooden legs. My, what a sight that was! The clothes horse still wore the collars and handkerchiefs that had been drying on it, and it did look funny. The enchanter was quite frightened to see such a strange creature, and forgot all the magic spells he knew till the pixies were halfway home.

They galloped right to Dame Twiddle's on the clothes horse, for it was time for the party. How everyone stared to see them coming on such a strange steed!

'Whoa, horse! Whoa there!' shouted Pompetty to the clothes horse, and the two pixies jumped off. Diddle was just about to tie it to the gatepost with some rope he had found when it tossed its funny head, whinnied loudly and galloped off to the west.

Nobody knows where it went to. Diddle thinks it will go to the moon and back again, and he hopes he will catch it once more when it comes back. But if I see it I shall catch it! Wouldn't you?

The Enchanted
Pencil

The Enchanted Pencil

NOBODY LIKED Nippy very much. He was a small, soft-footed goblin, and you couldn't leave anything about when he was near, in case he slipped away with it.

'Now where's my bag of groceries gone?' Dame Toddle would say. 'I just put it down on that chair for a moment – and then I look round and it's gone!'

So it had – and Nippy had gone with it. Nothing was safe near him, not even a box of matches. Into Nippy's pocket it would go. He had gone off with Mr Shabby's library book, Mother Rose's gloves, and a bag of sweets belonging to Tiny the pixie.

Nobody ever saw him take anything – but everybody knew!

'I can't go after him unless I have proof,' said Mr Plod the policeman. 'Can't accuse anyone without proof, you know. All I can say is be careful, all of you, and don't leave your things about!'

'We don't leave them about – we only put them down for a moment,' said Dame Toddle. 'I put my bag of groceries down to get out my purse, that's all, and lo and behold, it disappears in an instant!'

'We'll have to chain all our belongings to us,' said Mother Rose, gloomily. 'What he wants with my gloves I don't know. They wouldn't fit his big, bony hands.'

When Dame Sharp-Eye came to stay with Mother Rose, she heard all about Nippy. 'And really I don't know what we can do about him,' said Mother Rose. 'He's quite impossible.'

'Oh, I think I can manage to deal with him for you,' said Dame Sharp-Eye. 'You leave it to me.'

'Can you really?' said Mother Rose. 'That would be marvellous.'

Dame Sharp-Eye went and rummaged in her bag upstairs. She took out a little narrow box, rather long. In it was a pencil – a most peculiar one!

It was green and gold, and had a curious sharp point at the bottom of it, like the sting of an insect. When it wrote, the writing was beautiful – sharp, strong and black. It was a very smart pencil indeed.

'Ah, there you are, my little magic pencil,' said Dame Sharp-Eye, pleased. 'I'm glad I brought you with me. Now see you work your magic properly when you leave me.'

The pencil stood up by itself, waggled a bit and then dropped down again.

'You've plenty of magic still in you, although you're so old,' said Dame Sharp-Eye. 'Now, into my handbag you go – and keep quiet while you're there.'

She went down to Mother Rose. 'I've found what I wanted,' she said. 'Tomorrow morning we will go shopping together, and we will go somewhere that Nippy is sure to be. We shall see some fun in a short while!'

So the next day out they went with their shopping bags. They went to the baker's. Nippy wasn't there. They went to the butcher's and then to the grocer's. Ah – there he was, collecting his groceries.

Dame Sharp-Eye looked at him. What a mean, shifty little goblin!

Yes, he needed a lesson all right. She took out her shopping list and her strange green and gold pencil. She put the pencil down on the counter.

Nippy saw it at once. His eyes gleamed. What a pencil! He could sell that for a lot of money to Sly-One the enchanter.

Dame Sharp-Eye bought a great many things. Then she took up her pencil. 'Pencil, add up my bill,' she said, and hey presto, that pencil ran itself down the bill and wrote down a sum of money at the bottom.

Nippy's eyes nearly fell out of his head. Good

gracious! It wasn't only an unusually beautiful pencil, but a magic one, too. He really must get hold of it.

Dame Sharp-Eye put the pencil down on the counter again and turned her back on it to look at some plums in a box nearby. In a flash Nippy's long arm reached out and snapped up the pencil. It went into his pocket at once, and he was out of the door before Dame Sharp-Eye had turned round.

But her sharp eye had seen everything all right! There was a little mirror in the shop, and although she had her back to the counter, she had seen Nippy snatch up the pencil and run off with it. She smiled at Mother Rose.

'He's taken it,' she said. 'Now there'll be some fun!'

Well, before Nippy had gone far he felt something pricking him. What could it be? He put his hand into his pocket to see if he had a pin there, and he felt a sharp prick in his hand. Goodness – had he got a bee in his pocket or something?

He didn't know it was the sharp point on the end of

the pencil! He got a few more pricks before he reached home and couldn't think what they were.

He took the pencil out and looked at it gleefully. 'My word! You'll be worth a lot of money!' he said. 'This is a bit of luck! To think you can add up sums too. You can do all my bills for me.'

The pencil wriggled in his hand and gave him a dig with its sharp end. Nippy dropped it at once. 'Ooooh – so it was you that kept pricking me! You horrid thing! I'll take you to the enchanter Sly-One at once and get rid of you!'

But that pencil hopped off the table and took itself to the bare wall. It scribbled something there in large writing: *No, you won't! I'm staying here!*

Nippy stared at the writing in astonishment. What a very, very magic pencil this was!

'It's no good your being rude to me,' he said to the pencil. 'You're going to be sold to Sly-One the enchanter, and I'm taking you now!'

He made a dart at the pencil and it jabbed its sharp

end into his hand again. Nippy howled. 'Oh, you mean thing! You've got a sting!'

The pencil scribbled on the wall! *I only sting bad people. That's why I sting you!*

'Now you stop writing rude things about me,' said Nippy angrily. 'Suppose someone comes in and sees all that?'

He took a cloth and began to wipe off what the pencil had written. He went to the kitchen to rinse out the cloth. When he came back he stared at the wall in horror. The pencil had been doing a bit of writing again!

Nippy has got Mother Rose's best gloves in his top drawer. Isn't he a thief? the pencil had written. Nippy went pale. Good gracious! Had the pencil been looking into his drawers? There were a lot of things there that Nippy didn't want anyone to see.

He grabbed at the pencil again and caught it. The pencil stung him hard and he dropped it with a yell. 'I'll throw you in the fire next time I get you!' he shouted. The pencil at once went to write on the wall again.

Nippy is so afraid of me that he says he will throw me in the fire.

Rat-a-tat-tat! That was a knock at the door. Nippy stared in despair at the wall. Goodness, he couldn't possibly ask anyone in with that scribbling on the wall. He rushed to get a wet cloth again. Soon he had the writing washed away, and he went to open the door.

'Goodness – you've been long enough opening the door!' said little Nosy-One the imp. 'What's up?'

'Nothing,' said Nippy. 'What do you want? Come to pay me my bill?'

'No,' said Nosy-One. 'I've come to say I can't. You'll have to give me another week.'

'I can't possibly,' said Nippy. 'I've no money at all, and I've my own bills to pay.'

Nosy-One suddenly stared at the wall behind Nippy's head. Nippy felt most uncomfortable. Was that pencil writing anything else?

It was. It had written: *Nippy's got plenty of money in his left-hand drawer, and he's got a watch belonging to Father Timmy in the right-hand one. Shame on you, nasty Nippy!*

'Oooh – is that a magic pencil?' said Nosy-One, in amazement. 'Isn't it rude? Does it keep writing things like that about you? Have you really got Father Timmy's watch? Oooh, I'm glad I haven't got a pencil like that!'

And out he ran to tell Father Timmy that Nippy had got his watch, and to spread the news that there was a very rude magic pencil at work in Nippy's house.

Father Timmy was soon round there. The wall had again been washed clean, but the pencil was hovering about, ready to begin its scribbling at any minute. Nippy had tried swatting at it with the fly-swatter, but the pencil was really very good at dodging.

'Have you got my watch, Nippy?' demanded Father Timmy sternly.

'No,' said Nippy.

The pencil began writing in such a hurry that the words went all crooked:

Ooh! He's a storyteller as well as a thief! Look in the right-hand top drawer.

Father Timmy pushed Nippy aside and looked in the drawer. There was his watch. He looked sternly at the goblin.

'I'm going to Mr Plod about this.'

Good! wrote the pencil. *Fetch Mr Plod!*

Father Timmy went out, frowning. Nippy stood glaring at the pencil. 'Look here,' he said, 'will you please go away, back to your mistress, Dame Sharp-Eye?'

No, wrote the pencil. *I'm staying here for the rest of my life. It's a nice cottage – just what my mistress would like, too.*

'Well, either you go or I go,' said Nippy, and he hit out at the pencil again. It stung him and then wrote quickly:

Well, I'm staying. Goodbye!

And goodbye it was, because Nippy didn't dare to stay with that enchanted pencil, and neither did he want to meet Mr Plod if he came back with Father Timmy. So he packed his bag and caught the very next bus out of the village.

'Where's Nippy?' said Mr Plod, when he came along with Father Timmy and Dame Sharp-Eye, who was expecting something of the sort.

Gone for good! wrote the pencil.

'Splendid,' said Mr Plod. 'It will be a good riddance to bad rubbish. Well, I'll search the house and see what stolen goods there are. Then we'll sell the furniture and give the money to the many people Nippy has robbed. But what shall we do with the house?'

'It's just what I want,' said Dame Sharp-Eye at once. 'I came to stay with Mother Rose to look for a house here, Mr Plod. I want to live in this nice village. I'll have the house.'

'We shall be delighted to have the owner of this

remarkable pencil living in our village,' said Father Timmy. 'Do you agree, Mr Plod?'

'I certainly do,' said the policeman. 'I'm very, very grateful to you, Dame Sharp-Eye, for getting rid of that tiresome little nuisance. You shall certainly have this cottage as soon as ever it's ready.'

The pencil scribbled quickly on the wall. *Hurrah!* it wrote. *Three cheers! I like this place.*

Dame Sharp-Eye laughed. 'Well, pencil, you won't be allowed to write on the walls once I'm living here. You'll have to behave yourself.'

And the pencil wrote, *I will!*

Mr Wiggle's
Scissors

Mr Wiggle's Scissors

MR WIGGLE was a tailor who made a lot of money. He lived in Fiddle-Town, and he owned a marvellous pair of scissors that people came miles to see.

These scissors were made of pure gold, and had a magic spell in them. Wiggle had only to put them down on a piece of cloth and say 'Scissors, cut out a dress,' or 'Scissors, cut out a fine pair of trousers,' and at once the golden scissors would set to work. They saved Mr Wiggle a lot of time and trouble, besides giving him a great name for wonderful dress and tunic patterns.

Even the Queen of Fairyland had been known

to order a special dress from him. But Wiggle wasn't at all vain. He lived in his little cottage and worked hard week in and week out. There was just one thing he wanted and had never had – and that was a chance to be the chief brownie in Fiddle-Town and sit on the silver chair at all the town meetings.

But only clever brownies were allowed to do that, and although Wiggle was really a very thoughtful, wise brownie, he was so quiet that no one really thought of him as clever, and he was never voted for when a new chief brownie had to be chosen.

Now one day a strange piece of news went round Fiddle-Town. There was an empty house at the end of the village, and someone had taken it to live in and that someone was a witch! A witch in Fiddle-Town! That really was a most extraordinary thing, for witches did not usually come to live near brownies. Brownies hated witches and feared them.

This witch was well known. Her name was

Greeneye and you can guess why. She was a wicked, sly creature, always making up strange, cunning magic. She had been banished from the last town she had lived in, and when she heard of the empty house in Fiddle-Town she thought it would suit her well, and moved in the very next day.

'What are we going to do about Witch Greeneye?' asked the brownies at their next meeting. Mr Heyho, the chief brownie, sat in the silver chair and looked solemnly at everyone. Really, something would have to be done, he said. But nobody knew what!

'Well,' said Heyho, rising from his silver chair, 'if anyone thinks of a really good idea he had better be the next chief brownie, because I can't think of anything!'

Mr Wiggle the tailor went home and thought hard. Here was a chance for him to be chief – if only he could think of a good idea. He sat down in his rocking-chair and thought for quite twenty minutes.

And at the end of that time he smiled. He had thought of a plan.

His windows looked out on the back garden of the witch's house. Wiggle watched to see when the witch had her washing-day. On the next Tuesday he saw a great many clothes hanging out on the line.

He quickly put on his hat and went to call on the West Wind, who was a great friend of his.

'West Wind,' he said, 'will you do me a favour? There's a nasty old witch living just near my house and she has hung all her washing out on her line. Would you please go along and blow it all away and hide it for a little while where she can't find it?'

'But what for?' asked West Wind, in surprise.

'Never mind what for,' answered Wiggle. 'I've got a very good reason.'

'Very well,' said the wind, laughing. 'It will be a good joke. I'll go along and do it now.'

So when Greeneye the witch looked out of her kitchen window to see how her clothes were drying, she got a terrible shock – for West Wind had just that very minute blown along, and was sweeping every single one of her nicely washed clothes off the line.

Away they went, two dresses and two cloaks, three petticoats and a veil. West Wind blew them up the hill and down the other side. Greeneye raced after them, but when she got to the top they were nowhere to be seen. West Wind had hidden them away very cunningly.

'Oh, you villain,' cried Greeneye to the wind. 'You've stolen away all my clothes! Now I shall have to go and buy some more!'

That was just what Mr Wiggle the tailor wanted. He peeped through his window and was delighted to see the witch walking towards his shop. Soon she had opened the door and walked in.

'Hello, Mr Wiggle,' she called banging on the counter. 'Where are you? Don't keep me waiting.'

'Sorry,' said Wiggle, coming out of his workshop. 'I'm very busy, just at the moment!'

'Well, you may be busy, but you've got to put all your other work on one side and make me some dresses and a cloak,' snapped the witch. 'That wretched West Wind has stolen all the clothes off my line, and I must have some more. I want them by tomorrow.'

'I'm afraid that's impossible,' said Wiggle, politely. 'I've a tunic to finish for Heyho, the chief brownie, and a gown for Mrs Tiddlywinks, and a pair of trousers for her little boy.'

'Don't be silly,' said the witch, sharply. 'You must put everything on one side and make what I want! You don't want me to turn you into a black beetle for disobeying me, do you?'

'No, I don't,' said Wiggle, pretending to be frightened. 'But I really must finish these jobs first, Witch Greeneye. But I have an idea – perhaps if I lent you my magic scissors you could get them to cut out what you want, and then sew the things together yourself. It's the cutting out that is so difficult, isn't it? But if you had my scissors, you could easily get them to do the hard part for you, and then it wouldn't cost you much to have the things you want – you could just sew up the seams yourself.'

'That's a good idea,' said the witch, who was always pleased to save money when she could. 'Where are these scissors?'

'I'll go and get them,' said Wiggle, and he went into his workshop, grinning to himself. He picked up his golden scissors, and took half the spell out of them before he gave them to the witch. She didn't wait to thank him but went straight off to her house with them, planning all the dresses she would have.

She pulled some material from a box and spread it out on the table. Then she popped the scissors on it and commanded them to set to work. In a trice they opened themselves and began to cut the cloth out in the shape of a dress. The witch was delighted.

She laid out another piece of cloth and the scissors cut out a cloak for her. Then she thought she would sew up the dress and the cloak, and she put the scissors on her kitchen dresser. But how great was her surprise to hear them still clipping merrily away! She looked up and saw that they had jumped to the curtains and were busily cutting them out in the shape of a coat!

'You wicked things! Stop that at once,' cried the witch, in a rage. She caught hold of the scissors, but let them go with a shout for they quickly pricked her hand with their points. They flew to the tablecloth and began to cut it up in the shape of a pair of trousers. The witch was so angry that she hardly knew what to do.

She did not dare to touch the scissors again, but she quickly looked up all her magic books to see what words she should use to make them stop. But she could find nothing at all to help her. It was dreadful.

The scissors cut up the carpet next and then all the cushions in the chairs. Then they neatly cut up the kettle-holder and flew into the bedroom to see what they could do to the bedspread and sheets!

The witch followed them, shouting and crying with

rage, but it wasn't a bit of good. She simply could not stop those scissors! And, oh dear me, when they had finished cutting up everything they could, what do you think they did? They flew to the witch herself, and began to cut off her hair! Then they started to cut her clothes into rags, and poor Greeneye rushed out of the house in terror.

She ran to Mr Wiggle's and burst into his shop with the scissors busily cutting the laces of her boots.

'Mr Wiggle! What's wrong with these scissors? They won't stop cutting! Put the right spell into them at once, or I will turn you into an earwig.'

'Well, if you turn me into an earwig, those scissors will never leave you!' said Wiggle, sewing busily at a coat. 'Now, Witch Greeneye, let us talk together. I will tell you truthfully that I have taken half the spell from my scissors – and I don't mean to put it back again until you promise me something.'

'You wicked brownie! What do you want me to promise you?'

'You must promise me to pack your box and leave Fiddle-Town for ever,' said Wiggle, sewing on a button at top speed. 'We don't like you. You're cunning and sly. We would much rather have your room than your company.'

'Well, I shall stay!' shouted the witch in a terrible temper. 'I shall stay – and I shall make all sorts of terrible spells to punish you and the other brownies!'

'Well, the scissors will stay too,' said Wiggle. 'Be careful they don't cut off your nose. I see they've cut off your hair already.'

'Oh! Oh! Oh!' wailed the witch. 'What shall I do? Go away, you hateful scissors! Stop cutting, I tell you!'

But the scissors took not the slightest notice, and managed to snip off the toes of both her boots.

Suddenly Greeneye boxed Mr Wiggle's ear hard and ran out of his shop, the scissors following her. She went weeping to her house and packed all her things into three big boxes. Then she clapped her hands seven times and four broomsticks came flying through the air. The witch tied a box on each of the three biggest, and then sat herself on the smallest, with her big black cat behind her.

'Away! Away!' she cried. At once the broomsticks rose up into the air and Wiggle ran out to call all the brownies of Fiddle-Town to see the wonderful sight of Witch Greeneye really leaving the village at last.

'Hurrah! Hurrah!' they cried. 'How did you make her go, Mr Wiggle?'

'Come here, scissors!' shouted Wiggle. He was afraid that his magic scissors might follow the witch in her travels. The scissors flew down into his hand and he shut them. They stayed still and cut no more until he next commanded them. He knew the magic word to halt them in their work.

Wiggle told all the brownies what he had done, and called West Wind to ask him where he had hidden the witch's clothes. The West Wind blew them out of a cave on the other side of the hill. Wiggle packed them into a basket and bade the wind blow them after the witch.

'We don't want anything belonging to such a cunning creature left behind,' he said. 'Well, fellow brownies, I hope you approve of what I have done for you.'

'Clever old Wiggle!' shouted everyone, and they hoisted him up on their shoulders. 'You shall sit in the silver chair and be our chief brownie! Clever old Wiggle!'

Mr Wiggle was delighted. He sat down in the silver chair and beamed at everyone. It was the very proudest day of his life.

'Scissors, you must share my glory,' he said, and he took them from his pocket and set them on the seat beside him. Then everyone cheered madly, and the scissors were so alarmed that they jumped back into their master's pocket again.

No one knows what became of Witch Greeneye. It is said that her broomstick bumped into a thunderbolt and disappeared. It is certain that she was never seen again!

The Walkaway
Shoes

The Walkaway Shoes

'YOU KNOW, the two new brownies who have set up a shop in Toadstool Cottage make the most beautiful shoes,' said Pixie Light-Feet to Clumpy the gnome. 'You should get them to make you a pair of shoes for your poor old feet, Clumpy. Then you could walk well again.'

Clumpy went to see the two brownies, Slick and Sharpy. They bowed and smiled and welcomed him.

'Yes, yes, Clumpy. We will make you such a comfortable pair of shoes that you won't want to take them off even when you go to bed!' they said.

Well, they made him a red pair with green laces,

and they were so beautiful and so comfortable that Clumpy went around telling everyone about them.

Soon all the little folk of the village were going to Slick and Sharpy for their shoes, and the two brownies worked hard the whole day long. They were pleased.

'Our money-box is getting full,' said Slick. 'Is it time we did our little trick, Sharpy?'

'It is,' said Sharpy. 'Now, in future we put a walkaway spell into every pair of shoes. Don't forget!'

Dame Shuffle came that day and ordered a pair of blue boots. 'We've got just what you want!' said Slick, showing her a pair. 'Try them on!'

She tried them on, and they fitted her so well that she bought them at once, grumbling at the price. 'I'll wrap them up for you,' said Sharpy, and he took them into the other room to find some paper. He slipped a little yellow powder into each boot and then wrapped them up and took them to Dame Shuffle. Off she went, and wore them out to tea that afternoon.

'Beautiful!' said Mother Nid-Nod. 'I'll get a

pair from Slick and Sharpy, too.'

'So will I,' said Mr Tiptap. And the next day off they went to buy a pair each. But on the way they met Dame Shuffle, who looked very worried.

'Someone came in the night and stole my boots,' she said. 'My beautiful new boots that cost so much. They are quite, quite gone.'

'Oh dear – robbers must be about,' said Mr Tiptap. 'I shall be very careful of mine when I get them.'

He got a pair of red shoes and Mother Nid-Nod got a pair of brown shoes with green buckles. Slick and Sharpy grinned at one another when both customers had gone.

'Did you put the walkaway spell in them?' said Slick.

Sharpy nodded. 'Yes, both pairs will be back again tonight!' he said. 'And we'll put them into our sack ready to take away with us when our money-box is quite full.'

That night the spell inside Mother Nid-Nod's

brown shoes and Mr Tiptap's red ones began to work. Mother Nid-Nod heard a little shuffling sound and thought it was mice. She called her cat into her bedroom at once.

'Cinders,' she said, 'catch the mice in this room while I am asleep.' So Cinders watched – but instead of mice running about he saw Mother Nid-Nod's shoes walk to the door and all the way downstairs, and hop out of the open kitchen window. How scared he was!

Mr Tiptap's shoes did exactly the same thing. The old man didn't hear anything, he was so sound asleep. But the brown owl in the woods suddenly saw a pair of red shoes walking along all by themselves, and was so surprised that he almost fell off the branch he was sitting on.

'Who-who-who is that?' he hooted. 'Is there someone invisible walking in those shoes? Who-who-who is it?'

But it wasn't anyone, of course. It was just the

walkaway spell in the shoes sending them back to the two bad brownies. The people of the village began to get very upset. Everyone who bought lovely new shoes from Slick and Sharpy lost them in the night. And then, when they brought their old shoes to be mended and took them home again, those went too!

Slick and Sharpy just slipped walkaway spells in the mended shoes as well – and, of course, they walked away to the little toadstool house the very next night!

'Our money-box is full,' said Slick. 'Most of the shoes we have made for the people here have come back to us – as well as a lot of their old shoes that we mended.'

'Good,' said Sharpy. 'Let's go to another village now. We can settle in and do no work for a long time because we shall have so many pairs of boots and shoes to sell!'

'We'll just make this last pair of high boots for Mr Bigfeet,' said Slick. 'He has promised us five gold pieces for them – so that means we will have a lot of money from him and if we put the usual walkaway spell in the boots we shall have those, too, because they will come back to us tonight!'

Mr Bigfeet called for the boots that afternoon and paid for them. 'I hope no one comes to steal these boots!' he said. 'They're beautiful!'

Now, Bigfeet had a little servant called Scurry-About. She was a timid little goblin, very fond of her big master. She thought the boots were lovely, and she polished them till they shone that night.

'Oh, Master!' she said. 'I hope no one will steal them!'

'Well, see that they don't!' said Bigfeet and went up to bed. Scurry-About always slept down in the kitchen. The boots were there, too. She looked at them.

'Oh dear – I sleep so very soundly that if anyone comes to steal them I would never hear!' she said. 'I know what I'll do! I'll go to sleep wearing them! Then if a robber comes he will have to pull them off my feet and I shall wake up and scream!'

Well, she curled herself up in her small bed with the big boots on her feet. They reached right up to her knees! She fell sound asleep.

And in the night the walkaway spell began to work! The boots wanted to walk back to Slick and Sharpy. But they couldn't, because Scurry-About was wearing them. They began to wriggle and struggle to get themselves off her feet.

She woke up at once. 'Who's pulling off the boots? Master, Master, come quickly, someone is stealing your boots!' she cried.

Bigfeet woke up at once and came scrambling down to the kitchen. He was most surprised to find Scurry-About wearing his boots. And dear me, what was this? They leapt off her bed, taking her with them – and then began to walk to the window. Up to the sill they jumped, and then tried to leap out.

But Scurry-About was still in them, and she screamed because she was stuck halfway through the window. 'Help, help! The boots are taking me away!'

And then Bigfeet suddenly knew what was happening! 'There's a spell in them!' he cried. 'A walkaway spell, put there by those tiresome brownies – the rogues! Scurry-About, I'm going to open the window wide and let the boots take you away with them – but I'll follow close behind!'

'Oh, Master! Help me!' squealed poor little Scurry-About, and woke up all the villagers around, so that they threw on their dressing-gowns and came hurrying to see what was happening.

Bigfeet opened his window wide. The boots set off at top speed with Scurry-About's feet in them, taking her along too. Through the wood and into the lane and down the street – and right up to the front door of Toadstool Cottage went those big top-boots!

And there they kicked at the door to be let in. Scurry-About was crying, and Bigfeet was shouting in rage. All the other villagers were calling out in amazement.

'See! They are walking off to Slick and Sharpy! The

wicked brownies! Wait till we get hold of them!'

Slick and Sharpy heard all this and they were very frightened. Slick peeped out of the window. When he saw such an angry crowd he was alarmed.

'Quick, Sharpy,' he said. 'We must get out of the back door as soon as we can. Don't wait for anything – not even the money-box!'

So they fled down the stairs and opened the back door quietly. Out they went into the night and nobody saw them go.

The top-boots kicked the door down and everyone went inside the house. Scurry-About pulled off the boots, crying.

'They've gone,' said Bigfeet, looking all round.

'But they've left behind their money-box full of money – and sacks full of the boots they made for us!' said Mr Tiptap, emptying them out. 'Aha! It's our money because we paid it out to them – and they're our boots because they were made for us. How well-off we are!'

Nobody knew where Slick and Sharpy went to, and nobody cared. The villagers kept the boots and shoes and gave little Scurry-About two beautiful pairs for herself.

As for the money, it is being spent on a birthday present for the little Prince of Dreamland, who is five years old next week. He is going to have a box of big wooden soldiers, who march away in rows – and then walk back again! You see, Bigfeet found the walkaway spell in a box at Toadstool Cottage – so won't the little prince be surprised!

The Magician's Inkpot

The Magician's Inkpot

THE FAMOUS magician Dear-me lived in Crinkle Cottage with his little cook Ooh-my. She was the only servant that Dear-me had, except for a genie that came whenever he rubbed a magic ring he wore on his finger.

This genie would do anything the magician commanded. He would bring food, drink, dresses, gold, jewels – anything. Ooh-my's eyes nearly dropped out of her head when she saw what the genie could do. She wished she could have a genie of the ring too but no matter how much she rubbed her own little brass ring no genie appeared to do her bidding.

Now, one day the magician packed up his bag and

went away for a weekend, for he was rather tired. He left Ooh-my in charge of Crinkle Cottage, and told her to be sure and keep everything nice and clean. Then he said goodbye and went off to catch the bus.

Now the next morning, when Ooh-my was sweeping the floor, what should she find but a ring – and it was the very ring that the magician used to rub to make the genie come to do his bidding.

'Ooh my!' said Ooh-my. 'He must have dropped it without knowing! Ooh, it's the first time I've ever held it in my hands!'

She slipped it on her little finger, and then an idea came into her silly head. Why shouldn't she call up the genie herself, and set him to do some task? How grand it would be to feel as powerful as that!

Without stopping to think, she began to rub the ring with her duster. At once there was a loud crash, smoke filled the room, and there before her was the genie of the ring. But when he saw that it was not the magician who had called him, he did not bow low, as he usually did, but frowned deeply.

Ooh-my was frightened. She wished she hadn't used the ring. She didn't know what to say to the genie at all. So all she said was 'Ooh my! Ooh!'

'Tell me something to do!' commanded the genie in a booming voice. 'Quick! Tell me something to do, or I shall disappear and take you with me.'

'Ooh my!' groaned the little cook. 'What shall I tell him?'

'Quick!' commanded the genie impatiently. 'Set me a task.'

Ooh-my suddenly saw that the magician's inkpot was almost empty.

'Fill the inkpot with ink!' she said.

At once the genie took a large bottle from the air and began to fill the pot with ink. Ooh-my ran thankfully from the room. She couldn't bear to be with the genie any longer. She went to the kitchen and made herself a cup of hot, strong tea, for she was really feeling very upset.

She hadn't sat there more than twenty minutes when she began to wonder what the genie was doing. He must have filled the inkpot a long time ago. Perhaps he had done that and gone. Ooh-my hoped very much he had.

She made up her mind to go and see. So she left the kitchen and tiptoed to the parlour door; and, oh, dear me! Whatever should she see but the genie *still* pouring ink into the inkpot! Of course, it was quite full, running over. The ink had overflowed on to the new tablecloth and run to the floor. All the pretty carpet was soaked in ink, and a big stream of black was slowly making its way to the door where Ooh-my stood.

'Ooh my!' said the little cook, in horror. 'Ooh my! Whatever will the magician say? Just look at all that ink! Stop, genie, stop!'

But the genie took no notice of Ooh-my at all. He simply went on pouring out the ink from the endless bottle, and the black stream got bigger and bigger, till it swirled round Ooh-my's feet and made her brown shoes black.

She gave a shriek of dismay and tore back to the kitchen. But the ink followed her there, and soon her nice clean kitchen was all black and wet with ink.

'What shall I do? What shall I do?' wept Ooh-my. 'This is terrible! How can I get that genie away? He won't take any notice of what I tell him!'

The ink rose higher and higher, and at last Ooh-my opened the back door and went out, for she felt certain she would be drowned in ink if she didn't. The ink ran out down the path, and the passing gnomes and brownies stared in amazement.

And who should Ooh-my see coming down the road but the magician Dear-me himself! He had got tired of his holiday and had come back sooner than he had expected.

How glad Ooh-my was to see him! She ran up to him in a great hurry.

'Master! Master!' she cried. 'Come quickly! That genie of yours is filling the kitchen with ink, and I can't make him stop!'

The magician ran to his cottage. His feet squelched in the ink, and he was splashed with black from head to foot. When the genie saw him he stopped pouring out the ink and bowed very low.

The magician clapped his hands twice.

'Go!' he said. 'Vanish! Disappear! You are in disgrace!'

The genie vanished with a bang, and the room was filled with smoke again. Ooh-my waded in behind her master, crying bitterly as she saw all the damage that had been done.

'Where is my ring?' asked the magician. 'Give it to me. And remember this, Ooh-my – never meddle with my things again. I shall not punish you, because the mess you will have to clear up is punishment enough. Stop crying, and go and get pails of water.'

Ooh-my handed her master the ring, and wiped her

eyes. She went to get water from the pump, and all that day and the next she spent trying to get rid of the ink.

'I'll never – *never* – NEVER meddle with things that don't concern me again!' she vowed, as she scrubbed away at the black ink-marks. And, so the magician tells me, she never has!

Wizard
Grumpity-Groo

Wizard
Grumpity-Groo

THERE WAS a most unpleasant wizard called Grumpity-Groo. He settled down in the very middle of Fairyland, and nobody could get rid of him. Even the Fairy Queen herself could do nothing, and when she called one morning at the wizard's little cottage he was very rude to her.

'Good morning, madam, and goodbye,' he said, opening and shutting the door all in one movement. And that was all he said. Wasn't he rude?

Kimmy the elf was with the queen, and he was very cross that anyone should be so rude to her. So he quite lost his temper, and threw open one of the wizard's windows and gave him a good smack.

The wizard was angry. He pulled the elf into his cottage, shut the window with a bang, and then turned to Kimmy with a deep frown.

'You shall be taught a lesson,' he said. 'You shall be my servant for a year and a day.'

Poor Kimmy! He did have to work hard. He had to do all the work of the cottage, draw all the magic circles that the wizard wanted – and he needed a good many – stir the magic cauldron over the fire, and collect the herbs that Grumpity-Groo commanded him to find.

But all the time he was wondering how to defeat the wizard, who was really a very unpleasant fellow. He was much worse than the queen had guessed, and Kimmy was horrified at the things he did.

Then one day Grumpity-Groo began boasting that he was very clever.

'Oh, I'm the greatest wizard in the whole world!' he said. 'No one in Fairyland is so powerful as I!

One day I will catch the Fairy Queen and marry her. Then I shall be King of Fairyland, and do just what I like! I shall shut the fairies up into jars, and throw them to the bottom of the sea!'

'Oooh!' said Kimmy, very much afraid. 'But are you more powerful than the old witch Gloomy, who lives right at the other end of Fairyland?'

'Pooh!' said the wizard. 'Of course.'

'But she can do *wonderful* things!' said the elf. 'She can turn herself into a black cat whenever she likes!'

'So can I,' cried the wizard, and in a twinkling he vanished, and in his place was the largest black cat that Kimmy had ever seen. It came towards the elf, hissing and showing its large claws. Kimmy was frightened and ran into a corner. Then the cat laughed and in another moment it changed back to the wizard.

Then a wonderful idea came to the elf. He pretended to be scornful.

'That's nothing,' he said. 'Any old wizard could do that! Could you change yourself into a beetle with green spots and yellow stripes?'

'Easy!' cried the wizard, and in a flash he had disappeared, and in his place was a large beetle with green spots and yellow stripes, running across the floor.

Then it vanished and the wizard again appeared.

'Would you like me to do anything else to show my wonderful powers?' he asked.

'Yes,' said Kimmy boldly. 'Change yourself into a pound of sugar, and put yourself into that bag over there! I don't believe that any wizard could do a thing like that!'

Grumpity-Groo laughed loudly.

'You do give me easy things to do!' he said. 'Why, even a very young wizard could do that! Ask me something harder!'

'Ah, you only say that because you can't do it!' cried Kimmy.

The wizard frowned.

'You are bold to speak to me like this!' he growled.

'I will do as you say, and then when I change back to my own form, I shall punish you for being so rude to me.'

He vanished. The elf waited to see what would happen. On the floor appeared a heap of lump sugar, and then lump by lump it jumped into the bag on the table. When the last lump had gone inside, the elf rushed to the bag. He took a piece of string and tied it tightly round the neck – the wizard was a prisoner.

Kimmy rushed out of the cottage, and ran as hard as he could to the Fairy Queen's palace. The lumps of sugar jumped about like mad, but they couldn't get out and change back to the wizard because the elf had tied up the bag so tightly.

At last he arrived panting at the palace gate. He ran up the steps and begged to see the queen. In two minutes he was before her, and she was asking him what was the matter.

'I've got the wizard in this bag!' said Kimmy. 'What shall we do with him? He has changed himself into lumps of sugar.'

'But whatever made him do that?' asked the queen in astonishment. Quickly Kimmy told her all that had happened, and she was very glad when she heard how he had defeated the wicked wizard.

'But what shall we *do* with him now that we've got him?' asked Kimmy. 'We must think of something quickly, because I expect the sugar will make a hole in the bag by the way it is jumping about, and then, oh, dear me! He will change back to his old shape and punish us all most severely.'

The queen thought hard for a moment, then she called to an attendant.

'Bring a bowl of hot water!' she commanded. The attendant brought it and put it on a table by the Queen. Then with trembling hands Her Majesty opened the bag, turned it upside-down, and emptied all the sugar lumps into the water!

They made a curious sizzling sound and the water turned bright green.

'All the sugar will dissolve, and that will be the end of the wizard!' said the queen to the astonished elf. They watched the water. The lumps gradually fell to pieces, and soon there was nothing to be seen but the green water. Then it suddenly turned back to its right colour again, and the Queen gave a sigh of relief.

'That's the end of him!' she said. 'What a dreadful person he was! And how clever of you to think of such a good idea, Kimmy! I will give you ten bags of gold and a castle of your own. Then you will be rich for the rest of your life!'

She kept her word, and Kimmy became a very grand person indeed. He married and took his wife with him to his castle, and there they live happily to this very day!

Big-Eyes
the Enchanter

Big-Eyes
the Enchanter

BIG-EYES THE enchanter had found a most marvellous spell. It was made of moonshine, starlight, the roots of mountains, the footfalls of a weasel, the breath of a fish and the smell of rain. It was stirred up with a Hoodle-Bird's tail-feather and boiled on a piece of shining ice.

It was the most powerful spell in the world. It would make Big-Eyes the enchanter king of all the lands on Earth. He could do what he liked. Ah, what a time he would have!

Big-Eyes was not a pleasant fellow. He didn't like flowers, he didn't like animals, he hated children. He couldn't bear fairies, he spanked every elf he met, and he hated to hear anyone laughing.

'When I use my spell and make myself king of all the lands on Earth, I will destroy the flowers everywhere!' he cried. 'I will shut all the animals up underground, and I will make all the boys and girls work hard for me from the moment they are three years old. As for the fairies and the elves, the goblins and the pixies, I'll send the whole lot to the bottom of the sea. Ho, what a time I'll have!'

He looked at the spell. It was shimmering in a great blue cauldron, stirred by his servant, a big lad with a stupid, grinning face.

Then Big-Eyes looked in his book of magic. He wanted to find out exactly when the spell would work. At last he found what he wanted to know.

'This spell when made will only act on Midsummer Day at five o'clock in the morning,' he read. 'Aha! Then I'll set my alarm clock for half past four, and get the spell working at five exactly. Then thunder and lightning will come and when the spell has stopped everyone will be my slave!'

The night before Midsummer Day, the enchanter set his alarm clock to go off at half past four. Then he went to bed, full of excitement to think of all the power that would be his next day. His servant, the grinning lad, had been told to keep awake all night, and stir the spell to keep it sweet.

The enchanter had exciting dreams. He dreamt that he was a monarch on a golden throne, set with all the rare jewels of the world. He dreamt that not a single flower blossomed on the earth. He dreamt that all the puppies and kittens, chicks and ducklings, calves and lambs were hidden away from the sunshine deep in the heart of the earth. He dreamt that all the boys and girls no longer played but worked all day long for him.

Sweet dreams for the wicked enchanter! On he dreamt and on – and at last woke up. No alarm bell woke him – he woke up himself. He looked at the clock. It was half past three.

Not time to get up yet. He lay and waited. Then he looked at the clock again, when about half an hour had gone.

It was still half past three. What a strange thing! The enchanter listened for a moment – and he could hear no ticking! The clock had stopped at half past three in the morning. He had forgotten to wind it up in his excitement the night before!

The village clock began to strike outside. One-two-three-four-five-six! Six o'clock! The right minute for the working of the spell was past! It wouldn't come again until a year was past!

In a fearful rage the enchanter sprang out of bed. Why hadn't the servant lad warned him, when the clock had stopped? He was supposed to keep awake all night and stir the blue cauldron!

The boy was fast asleep, poor lad, his head resting on the cauldron. Big-Eyes took him by the shoulder and shook him in fury. The boy woke up in fright, and, thinking that the enchanter was a thief come in the night, he struck out with all his might.

Biff! The enchanter fell to the ground, and as he fell he caught at the cauldron to save himself. Sizzle-sizzle-sizzle! The shimmering spell inside upset all over him as he lay on the ground.

The servant lad watched in terror. What would his master do to him now? He would beat him, surely, or at least turn him into a frog or beetle.

The spell acted strangely. It altered the enchanter bit by bit. He changed slowly into an old man – an old ragged man with a long ragged beard and bald head. He became a beggar-man, and slowly rose from the ground and went out to stand at a corner to beg from the passers-by. And little children were sorry for him and gave him pennies.

Sometimes he remembered how he had been a great enchanter, and then he would shake his head and mutter: 'Ah! I could have ruled the world! But I forgot to wind up the clock!'

As for the servant lad, what became of him? He got such a terrible fright that he ran off to sea, and one day he told this story to me. At the end he shook his head and said: 'Ah, it was a good thing my master forgot to wind up his clock that night!'

And dear me, I think it was too!

Whiskers and the Wizard

Whiskers and the Wizard

THERE WAS once a wizard called Blunder. He was the youngest and smallest of all the wizards, and he was not very good at learning magic.

He made so many mistakes that all the other wizards laughed at him.

'One of these days you'll cast a magic spell on yourself by mistake,' they said, 'and then you'll be in a fine pickle!'

But Blunder wouldn't listen to any advice. He thought he knew everything.

He carried on making spells, stirring up strange recipes for magic in his boiling cauldron, and muttering enchanted words to himself.

He had one servant – a faithful little rabbit called Whiskers. Most wizards, like witches, have cats for servants, for cats are wise and can keep secrets. But magic cats cost a great deal of money and Blunder couldn't afford one. So he had a rabbit instead, which was much cheaper.

Whiskers was a very clean and tidy servant. He swept and dusted, cooked and mended and looked after Blunder very well indeed. Sometimes he stirred the cauldron himself, though he was afraid of what magic might come out of it.

When he saw that Blunder often made mistakes, he was worried in case the little wizard should harm himself. He was very fond of his master, and wouldn't have let anything happen to him for all the world. So one day Whiskers asked if he could look at all the magic books. That way he thought he might learn some magic himself, and perhaps be able to help Blunder one day. But Blunder just laughed at him.

'Why, you're only a rabbit!' he said. 'You'll never be able to learn any magic. But you can look at my magic books if you like.'

So Whiskers waited until his work was done. Then he took down the magic books one by one, and read them all. He had a good memory, and very soon he knew a great many spells, and could say hundreds of magic words.

One day he saw Blunder mixing spiders' webs, blue mushrooms and the yolk from a goose's egg, chanting as he went:

'Tick-a-too, fa-la-lee,
Ta-ru, ta-ru, ta-roo,
Dickety, hickety, jiminy-japes,
Bibble and scribble and boo!'

'Master! Master!' cried Whiskers, dropping his broom in a hurry. 'You're saying the wrong words! Instead of making magic to grow a goose that lays golden eggs, you are saying a spell that will turn you into a goose yourself!'

It was true! Blunder had made a mistake. Already feathers had begun to sprout from his shoulders! Hurriedly he began to chant the right spell, and the feathers slowly disappeared.

But instead of being grateful to Whiskers, he was cross with him!

'I'd soon have found out my mistake!' he said sharply. 'Get on with your work, Whiskers, and in future don't interfere in things that you know nothing about.'

The next day, the powerful Wizard of Woz came to tea, but he arrived with bad news.

'The wicked goblin has been seen again in Pixie Wood,' said the old wizard. 'So we want *you* to get rid of him, Blunder. Or better still, make some magic that will get him into our power. Then we can make him into a useful servant. You know how to do it, don't you?'

'Of course I do!' said Blunder. 'You can trust me to do a simple thing like that! The goblin will be in your power before midnight.'

Blunder set to work as soon as the wizard had gone. He mixed together green elderberries, a small moonbeam, two thorns from a blue rose, and a drop of honey. Then he had to count from ninety-nine back to one, and stir all the time from left to right.

'Ninety-nine, ninety-eight, ninety-seven,' began Blunder and he had almost got to twenty, when Whiskers gave a cry of fear.

'Master! You're stirring the wrong way! Oh dear, oh dear, you'll put yourself in the goblin's power, instead of getting him into yours!'

Blunder stopped stirring in fright and began stirring the other way – but you can't do that sort of thing in the middle of a powerful spell! Something is bound to happen, and all of a sudden it did! There was a tremendous BANG and a blue-green flame shot out of the cauldron and whizzed twice around the room. Then it turned into a swirling purple wind that whisked Blunder up into the air and out of the window!

Whiskers crouched in a corner and waited for something else to happen. But nothing did – except that he heard a very strange laugh from somewhere that made him shiver and tremble.

'That was the goblin!' thought the little rabbit. 'He knows that Blunder has put himself in his power, and he's come to get him. Oh dear, I must try to rescue him at once!'

Meanwhile Blunder had flown out of the window, risen as high as the clouds, and then come down, bump, in a place he didn't know!

'This is a fine thing!' he said. 'Now what am I to do?' But at that moment he heard a horrid laugh, and suddenly there in front of him stood the wicked little goblin.

'Ho ho!' said the goblin. 'Now you're in *my* power, Blunder. You don't deserve to be a wizard when you make such silly mistakes. Come along, I'm going to keep you in my cave and you can be my servant!'

'Never!' cried Blunder. 'I won't go.'

But the goblin knew a little magic too. He muttered a few strange words, and at once Blunder's feet began to walk in the direction that the goblin wished them to.

'You will stay here until I get back,' said the wicked goblin when they had reached his cave. 'And just in case you try to misbehave, this will stop you.'

He drew a white chalk circle right around poor Blunder who watched him in dismay, for he knew that the circle was a magic one and would stop him using any spells to escape.

'Please set me free,' Blunder begged.

But the goblin would not listen. He just clapped his hands seven times, laughed and disappeared. At the same time a great stone rolled over the entrance to the cave, leaving Blunder all alone in the cold and dark.

'No one but Whiskers knows I am gone!' he wept. 'And how will he be able to help me? He's only a silly little rabbit.'

Little did Blunder know at that very moment Whiskers was busy searching for him. He had just reached the edge of Goblin Land and was trying to decide which way to go first.

'Now what I need is that spell I read the other day,' muttered Whiskers to himself. 'That will help me find my master.'

Soon he had remembered what to do. He took five green leaves and put them in a circle with their ends touching. Then he found a white feather and blew it into the air, singing the magic words as he did so. When he looked down again, the leaves had vanished! But the feather was still floating in front of him, floating away to the west as if blown by a strong breeze.

'Lead me to my master!' cried the rabbit, and followed the feather as it danced off down the hillside.

Soon it brought Whiskers to the cave. As soon as the little rabbit saw the great stone at the entrance he felt certain that his master was imprisoned behind it.

'Master, Master!' he called out. 'Are you there? It's me, Whiskers.' Inside the cave, Blunder could not believe his ears.

'Oh, Whiskers, is it really you!' he cried. 'I have been trapped in here by the wicked goblin. Can you help me escape? Can you move the stone?'

But even though Whiskers pushed against the great stone with all his strength, he could not move it even one inch.

'Never mind,' said the little wizard, in despair. 'Even if you could move it, it wouldn't be much use, for I can't move out of this magic circle. And even if I knew how to do that, I can't remember the spell that would get rid of the goblin's power.'

'Perhaps I can help,' cried the little rabbit. 'I think I can remember the spell about goblins.' And he started to recite it carefully to Blunder.

'That's just the one I want!' cried Blunder. 'Oh, Whiskers! If only you could gather all the ingredients together, I might be able to escape. But I'm afraid it's quite impossible.'

'Why's that?' said Whiskers in dismay.

'Because the final ingredient is a hair from my head,' explained Blunder. 'So unless we can move this stone, I'm stuck. I shall have to be that horrid goblin's slave for ever.'

Whiskers pushed at the great stone again, but it was no use. Then he had a brilliant idea! Wasn't he a rabbit? Couldn't he burrow like all rabbits do?

At once he began to burrow into the hillside, just beside the cave entrance. He sent out the earth in great showers, and in minutes he had made a tunnel into the cave where Blunder sat.

'Hurray!' cried Blunder. 'You're quite the most brilliant rabbit in the whole world. Now we can get to work.'

The little wizard knew that the one thing that could

destroy the goblin's power was the sight of a red, frilled dragon. And the spell told them exactly how to make one. So all that day and all that night brave little Whiskers went in and out of his tunnel, fetching nightshade berries, white feathers, blue toadstools, sunbeams, moonbeams and everything else that Blunder needed.

Soon all the ingredients were neatly piled at one end of the enormous cave. Whiskers put the last one on the very top and then sat down with his master to wait for the goblin to return.

Early the next morning they heard the goblin outside the cave. He shouted a magic word, and the stone flew away from the entrance. Then he strode in. Whiskers had hidden himself, and Blunder was pretending to be asleep.

'Ho ho! Ha ha!' said the goblin. 'What about a nice hot breakfast, Blunder? You must be hungry by now.'

The wizard pretended to groan.

'Well, tell me a few secret spells and I will give you

some toast and eggs,' said the goblin.

'Here is one,' said Blunder, raising his head, and he began to chant the spell that would turn all the magic things at the end of the cave into a fearful frilled dragon! The goblin listened carefully, grinning all the while because he thought that he was hearing a wonderful new spell.

Then, just as Blunder got to the last words, a strange thing happened. A rushing, swishing noise came from the end of the cave, and suddenly a dreadful bellow rang out. Then two yellow eyes gleamed, and lo and behold! A great dragon came rushing out!

'A frilled dragon!' yelled the goblin in fright. 'Oh my! Oh my! A great, red frilled dragon! Let me out! Let me go!'

And the goblin leapt six feet into the air, turned into a puff of smoke, and streamed out of the cave with the dragon after him. Whiskers and Blunder followed, and the last they saw of the wicked goblin was a thin cloud of smoke way up in the eastern sky.

The dragon soon gave up the chase, and turned back towards the cave. 'Quick!' whispered Whiskers. 'Change him into something else or he will eat us too!'

Blunder clapped his hands twice, and uttered a command. The dragon began to shrink, and when it was as small as a football it turned into a mass of red flames.

Whiskers hurriedly filled a jug with water and gave it to Blunder, who threw it over the flames – and sizzle-sizzle-sizzle, they went out! Nothing was left of the frilled dragon except for a few wet ashes.

'My goodness,' said Blunder, sitting down on the ground with a sigh. 'We have been having too many adventures, Whiskers. I shall be glad to get home, and sleep in my soft bed!'

'Poor Master, you must be very tired,' said the kind rabbit. 'Jump up on my back, and I'll take you home before you can say "Tiddley-winks"!'

So Blunder climbed up on Whiskers' soft back, and very soon he was safely home.

'Thank you very much for all you have done for me,' said the little wizard, hugging the delighted rabbit. 'I think you are much cleverer than I am, Whiskers. From now on you shall be my partner, not my servant, and you shall wear a pointed hat like me! We will do all our spells together, and then perhaps I shan't ever make a mistake again!'

Whiskers was so pleased.

'Well, let's go to bed now and have some sleep,' said Blunder, yawning. 'I can hardly keep my eyes open. Then tomorrow, we will go and buy your pointed hat.' So they both fell asleep, and Whiskers dreamt happily of wearing a pointed hat and helping Blunder with his spells.

Many years have passed since Blunder had his adventure with the wicked goblin. Whiskers is still with him, but now Blunder is very old, and Whiskers' ears have gone grey with age.

Sometimes when all their work is done, they sit one on each side of the fireplace, and Whiskers says: 'Do you remember that time when you made a mistake in your spells?'

Then they both laugh loudly, and wonder where the wicked goblin went to – for he has never been heard of from that day to this.

Acknowledgements

All efforts have been made to seek necessary permissions.

The stories in this publication first appeared in the following publications:

'Too-Wise the Wizard' first appeared in *Sunny Stories for Little Folks*, No. 78, 1929.

'The Little Pixie-Cat' first appeared in *Sunny Stories for Little Folks*, No. 170, 1933.

'The Strange Umbrella' first appeared in *Sunny Stories for Little Folks*, No. 121, 1931.

'Redcap and the Broomstick Witch' first appeared in *The Teacher's Treasury*, Vol. 1, 1926.

'Bobadil Becomes a Wizard' first appeared in *Sunny Stories for Little Folks*, No. 26, 1927.

'The Gobble-Up Witch' first appeared in *Sunny Stories for Little Folks*, No. 26, 1927.

'Mr Woff and the Enchanter' first appeared in *Sunny Stories for Little Folks*, No. 225, 1935.

'Buttercup Magic' first appeared in *Sunny Stories for Little Folks*, No. 73, 1929.

'The Wizard's Pink Cloak' first appeared as 'Pink! Pink!' in *Enid Blyton's Magazine*, No. 9, Vol. 2, 1954.

'The Dog that Helped a Fairy' first appeared in *Sunny Stories for Little Folks*, No. 234, 1936.

'The Page that Blew Away' first appeared in *Enid Blyton's Sunny Stories*, No. 498, 1951.

'Little Marya and the Witch' first appeared in *Sunny Stories for Little Folks*, No. 14, 1927.

'Mighty-One the Wizard' first appeared in *Sunny Stories for Little Folks*, No. 173, 1933.

'Mr Hoo-Ha's New Suit' first appeared in *Enid Blyton's Sunny Stories*, No. 51, 1937.

'It's Going to Rain!' first appeared in *The Teacher's World*, No. 1,724, 1936.

'The Enchanted Forest' first appeared in *Sunny Stories for Little Folks*, No. 153, 1932.

'The Sulkabit Wizard' first appeared in *Sunny Stories for Little Folks*, No. 16, 1927.

'Gee up, Old Clothes Horse!' first appeared as 'Gee-Up, Old Clothes Horse!' in *Enid Blyton's Sunny Stories*, No. 77, 1938.

'The Enchanted Pencil' first appeared in *Enid Blyton's Sunny Stories*, No. 441, 1948

'Mr Wiggle's Scissors' first appeared in *Sunny Stories for Little Folks*, No. 141, 1932.

'The Walkaway Shoes' first appeared in *Enid Blyton's Sunny Stories*, No. 527, 1952.

'The Magician's Inkpot' first appeared in *Sunny Stories for Little Folks*, No. 104, 1930.

'Wizard Grumpity-Groo' first appeared in *Sunny Stories for Little Folks*, No. 98, 1930.

'Big-Eyes the Enchanter' first appeared in *Sunny Stories for Little Folks*, No. 180, 1933.

'Whiskers and the Wizard' first appeared as 'Very-Young the Wizard' in *Sunny Stories for Little Folks*, No. 86, 1930.

Join the Adventure
THE FAMOUS FIVE

Five on a Treasure Island

Five Run Away Together

Five Go to Smuggler's Top

Five Go Off in a Caravan

Five on Kirrin Island Again

Five Go Off to Camp

Five Get into Trouble

Five Fall Into Adventure

Have you read them all?

More classic stories from the world of

Enid Blyton

The Famous Five Colour Short Stories

Enid Blyton also wrote eight short stories about the
Famous Five. Here they are, in their original texts,
with brand-new illustrations. They're a perfect
introduction to the gang, and an exciting new way to
enjoy classic Blyton stories.

Do you want to solve a mystery?

Enid Blyton

The Secret Seven

Join Peter, Janet, Jack, Barbara, Pam, Colin, George
and Scamper as they solve puzzles and mysteries,
foil baddies, and rescue people from danger – all without
help from the grown-ups. Enid Blyton wrote fifteen
stories about the Secret Seven. These editions contain
brilliant illustrations by Tony Ross, plus extra
fun facts and stories to read and share.